"Seen enough," he murmured, and she who never blushed felt warmth creep up her neck and along her cheeks.

"I think so." Cursing his appeal, and her blatant reaction to it, Madeline turned her attention back to the table. "Where were we?"

"No idea," he said. "But I think we should get it over with. It'd speed things up, and seeing as I'm only here for a week…"

"Get what over with?"

"Our first kiss." They were side by side, shoulder to shoulder.

"I do know my way around a man's mouth," she murmured. "Thing is, I'm not altogether sure *why* I'd want to kiss a man who despises me."

Accidentally educated in the sciences, **KELLY HUNTER** has always had a weakness for fairy tales, fantasy worlds and losing herself in a good book. Husband...yes. Children...two boys. Cooking and cleaning...sigh. Sports... no, not really, in spite of the best efforts of her family. Gardening...yes—roses, of course. Kelly was born in Australia and has traveled extensively. Although she enjoys living and working in different parts of the world, she still calls Australia home. Visit Kelly online at www.kellyhunter.net.

Kelly has been a RITA® Award finalist in the Best Cotemporary Series Romance category in both 2008 and 2010, with her novels *Sleeping Partner* and *Revealed: A Prince and a Pregnancy*.

UNTAMEABLE ROGUE
KELLY HUNTER

~ Rogues & Rebels ~

TORONTO • NEW YORK • LONDON
AMSTERDAM • PARIS • SYDNEY • HAMBURG
STOCKHOLM • ATHENS • TOKYO • MILAN • MADRID
PRAGUE • WARSAW • BUDAPEST • AUCKLAND

Recycling programs
for this product may
not exist in your area.

ISBN-13: 978-0-373-52792-2

UNTAMEABLE ROGUE

First North American Publication 2010.

Copyright © 2010 by Kelly Hunter.

www.eHarlequin.com

Printed in U.S.A.

Dear Reader,

They say that behind every great man there's a great woman.

The phrase is an old one, and I like the inherent equality in the statement. It's nice. There's room to maneuver. It doesn't imply that the strengths of men and women must be equal in every way, but there's balance there nonetheless. Balance is something I think about a lot when putting heroines and heroes together on the page.

My philosophy is not exactly brain surgery. I try to give my couples complementary strengths, and I'm all for balancing the equality equation. If my hero regularly saves the world, my gal's going to need resilience aplenty and the strength to let him do it. If my heroine's extremely wealthy, my hero had best be bringing something equally valuable to the relationship. Honor. Integrity. Acceptance. Balance.

What else do I think about when putting characters together on the page? I think about letting them have some fun, and I remember a Jim Carrey line from the film *Bruce Almighty*. I like the inherent playfulness in the statement. It's fun. Open to interpretation. It's also not a bad way to open a story.

The line?

"Behind every great man is a woman rolling her eyes."

I hope you enjoy *Untameable Rogue*.

Kelly Hunter

CHAPTER ONE

MADELINE MERCY DELACOURTE quite liked looking at near-naked men. She had her favourites, of course. Smooth-skinned willowy young men were easy on the eye and heaven knew Singapore was full of them. Well-preserved older men could also command attention on occasion, although general consensus had it that they were far easier to admire when they kept their clothes *on*.

No, for Madeline's money—and she had plenty of money—by far the most appealing type of near-naked man was the hardened warrior, complete with battle scars and formidable air. The ones who wore the *gi*—the loose martial arts robes—as if they'd been born to them. The ones who didn't bother with shirts in Singapore's sultry heat. Instead they let their glistening skin caress the air and please the eyes of those who knew where to find them.

Right now, as Madeline's eyes adjusted to the dim interior of the shabby little dojo in the heart of Singapore's Chinatown, she had the definite pleasure of happening upon not one shirtless warrior, but two.

The first was Jacob Bennett, a raven-haired steely-eyed Australian who'd found his way to Singapore around

the same time Madeline had—over ten years ago now—
and never left. They understood each other, she and Jacob.
Survivors both, no questions asked. This was his dojo
Madeline was standing in and if he had a softer side to
his formidable façade, well, she'd never seen it. He'd
scowl when he saw her. He always did. That was what
came of asking a kind man one too many favours.

Madeline had never seen Jacob's opponent before.
Not in the dojo, not in Singapore. She'd have remembered
if she had. He had an inch or so on Jacob when it came
to height, but when it came to muscle mass and the way
it wrapped around bone the men looked remarkably
similar. Same cropped black hair and skin tone too. A
brother perhaps, or a cousin, and certainly no stranger to
the martial arts. He had Jacob's measure, and that was
saying something.

They had the long sticks out, the Shaolin staffs, and
they fought with the grace of dancers and the ferocity of
Singapore's famous Merlion. Each man appeared intent
on annihilating the other but where Jacob was ice, his
opponent was fire. Less contained, thoroughly unpredictable. Reckless, even.

Reckless warriors were her favourite kind.

Jacob saw her and scowled. Madeline blew him a kiss.

'Is that him?' said the ragamuffin boy standing
beside her.

'That's him.'

'He doesn't look pleased to see us.'

'He'll get over it.'

Jacob's opponent must have heard them speaking or
followed Jacob's gaze, for he looked their way as well.

Bad move. Moments later the unknown warrior landed flat on his back, swept off his feet by Jacob's long stick. Madeline winced.

Jacob looked their way again and he really should have known better because the moment he took his eyes off his fallen opponent the warrior struck and Jacob too went down. A heartbeat later, each man had his hand wrapped around the other's throat.

'He looks busy,' said the boy. 'We should come back later.'

'What? And miss all this?' Besides, she figured the warriors were just about done. With a reassuring smile in the boy's direction, Madeline sauntered over to the two men, the heel of her designer shoes satisfyingly staccato against the scarred wooden floor. She crouched beside the warring pair and poked the mystery man's sweat-slicked shoulder with her fingernail, barely resisting the urge to trace a more lingering path. 'Excuse me. So sorry to interrupt. Hello, Jacob. Got a minute?'

The mystery man had expressive amber-coloured eyes; the predominant expression in them at the moment being one of incredulity. But his grip on Jacob's throat loosened and Jacob stopped sparring altogether and raised his hands in the universal gesture of surrender. Madeline smiled and offered the mystery warrior her hand, primarily to ensure he removed it from around Jacob's neck. 'Madeline Delacourte. Most people call me Maddy.'

'Often they just call her mad,' rasped Jacob.

'Flatterer,' said Madeline.

The warrior's eyes lightened and he smiled a dangerously charming smile as he rolled away from Jacob and offered up a warm and calloused hand. 'Luke Bennett.'

'A brother?' And at his nod, 'Thought so. You fight very well. Tell me, Luke Bennett…' she said as she withdrew her hand and rose from her crouching position. Both men followed suit and got to their feet, seemingly none the worse for the bruising. 'Which one of you wins these fearsome little encounters? Or do you both pass out at around the same time?'

'It varies,' said Luke. 'I can hold my breath for longer.'

'Handy,' murmured Madeline. He really did have the most amazing coloured eyes. 'And Jacob's advantage?'

'Stubbornness.' Those golden eyes took on a speculative light. 'But then, you probably already know that about him.'

Madeline smiled non-committally. She was, after all, about to ask the stubborn man a favour. She dragged her gaze away from Luke Bennett and focused on Jacob instead. Jacob's eyes were a bright piercing blue. It was like trading old gold for a slice of midday sky. 'I hear you're looking for a new apprentice.'

'You heard wrong,' said Jacob, his gaze sliding to Po, still hovering just inside the doorway. 'Besides, the last one you found for me stole everything that wasn't nailed down and most of the things that were.'

'He gave it all back, didn't he?' countered Madeline. '*And* he became your best student and won an Asian championship or ten for you.'

'Yeah,' said Jacob dryly. 'Right before the Hong Kong film industry came knocking and filled his brain with bright lights and tinsel.'

'See? I *knew* you needed a new apprentice.' Madeline bestowed upon him her most winning smile. 'Hey, Po. Come and meet the sensei.'

Po headed towards them warily. Small boy, somewhere in his early teens as far as Madeline could tell. That particular piece of information had never come her way and neither had Po's surname. For Po there was the street and his ability to survive on it, nothing more. It had taken Madeline six months to get the boy to even *consider* that there might be other lifestyle options open to him.

Jacob sighed heavily. 'Why me?' he muttered.

'Because you're a good man?' offered Madeline helpfully. 'Because if I put this one with anyone else he really will rob them blind?'

'You could always put him back where you found him,' offered Jacob. 'You can't save them all, Maddy.'

'I know.' But she could save some. And Jacob had been known to help her. 'Po's a pickpocket who works Orchid Road Central. He has a talent for annoying dangerous people. He needs to move on.'

'Why am I not surprised?' Jacob gave Po his full attention. 'Do you even *want* to learn karate, kid?'

Po shrugged. 'I want to live.'

'Can't argue with that,' said Luke Bennett cheerfully.

'You take him, then,' said his brother.

'Sorry.' Luke's lips curved unrepentantly and Madeline suddenly found herself ensnared by a man in a way she hadn't been for years. Rapid heartbeat, a curling sensation deep in her belly, an irresistible urge to bask in the warmth of that lazy smile—the whole catastrophe. 'You're the upright citizen. I'm the homeless one with the specialised skill set. I'd only corrupt him.'

'What exactly is it that you do?' Madeline asked.

'Mostly I examine sea mines and weaponry for the military.'

'Mostly when they're about to go boom,' added Jacob dryly. 'Life expectancy is a problem.'

'What's life without risk?' countered Luke with a glance in her direction. Amber eyes could be warm, she discovered. As warm as a lazy smile.

'I'm guessing that particular line of reasoning works for you a lot,' she said. 'I'm guessing you're inclined to categorise women into two main groupings. Those who run screaming when you smile at them and say that. And those who don't.'

Jacob guffawed, never mind that it landed him on the receiving end of a flat golden glare.

'This way, kid,' he said, still grinning as he turned and strode towards the far door. 'I offer a room with a bed and a pillow, one set of linen, provisions for three square meals a day, and below minimum wage. In return I require loyalty, obedience, honour and dedication from you. If you're not interested, feel free to go out the way you came in.'

Jacob didn't turn to see whether Po had chosen to follow him. Jacob knew street kids. He knew the boy would follow, if only to see if there was anything worth stealing later.

Luke Bennett watched Po and his brother walk away, his expression a mixture of exasperation and reluctant pride. Madeline watched Luke. It wasn't a hardship.

'You do this to him often?' he asked, turning and catching her examining him. She didn't blush.

'Often enough.'

'Do they stay?'

'Often enough.'

'Are you in love with my brother?'

'That's a very personal question.' Not one she felt inclined to answer. 'Why do you ask?'

'Jake doesn't let down his guard very often. He let it down for you.'

Madeline shook her head. 'The outer perimeter, maybe.' But Jacob Bennett's heart was locked down tight and Madeline knew with blind feminine instinct that she didn't hold the key to it. 'What would you do if I said yes?'

'Lament,' he said. And on a more serious note, 'I don't poach.'

'How very honourable of you. But then, I'd expect nothing less from a brother of Jacob's. Tell him I had to be going.'

'And my question?'

Madeline considered him thoughtfully, knowing the question for what it was. A declaration of interest, an invitation to play. She'd taken only one lover in the six years since William's death. She'd still been grieving, and in retrospect she'd wanted the comfort that came of intimacy far more than she'd wanted her lover's love. He'd wanted a woman he could honour and respect. It hadn't turned out well.

What would Luke Bennett look for in a lover? she wondered. Passion? Passion hadn't touched her in such a long time. Laughter? She could do somewhat better there. Honesty? She could give him that too, for what it was worth.

And then there was honour, and that she could not do.

'How long are you staying in Singapore, Luke Bennett?'

'A week.'

'Not long.'

'Long enough,' he countered. 'A person can pack a lot into a week if they try.' He shot her a crooked smile. 'You still haven't answered my question.'

'Only because I don't want to. Consider it one of life's little mysteries.'

'I hate mysteries,' he said. 'Fair warning.'

Hard not to smile a little at that. 'Enjoy your stay in Singapore, Luke Bennett. There's plenty to entertain.'

'There certainly is,' he murmured.

'There's plenty of things you'd do well to avoid too.' Fair warning. Smiling wryly, Madeline turned on her heel and let herself out.

'So what's the deal with you and Madeline Delacourte?' Luke asked his brother as they resumed their battle with the Shaolin sticks some fifteen minutes later, this time with a watchful pickpocket for an audience. 'You into her?'

'Why the interest?' asked Jake and followed through with a glancing blow to Luke's side.

Luke stopped talking and started concentrating on his defence. But the image of Madeline Delacourte—she of the knowing smile, honey-blonde hair, and long shapely legs—just wouldn't go away. 'Why do you think? I'm not asking for a kidney here. All I want is a straight yes or no answer from one of you.' He really didn't think it was too much to ask.

'No,' said Jake, blocking Luke's next blow. 'She's just a friend.'

'Is she married?'

'Not any more.'

'Engaged?'

'No.'

'Attached?'

'No.' Jake's stick caught him on the knuckles and damn near took his fingers off. 'Madeline's choosy. She can afford to be.'

'She's wealthy?'

'Very. Her late husband's family were British spice traders, back when the East opened up. They made a fortune and sank most of it into real estate. Maddy's husband owned a string of shopping centres and hotels along Orchid Road and half the residential skyscrapers in south-east Singapore. Maddy owns them now.'

'Her husband died young?'

'Her husband died a happy old man.'

Luke winced. He didn't like the picture Jake was painting. 'Any kids?'

'No.' More blows reached him. 'You're not concentrating,' said Jake.

'I'm still coming to grips with the trophy-wife thing.'

'Maybe she loved him.'

'How much older was he?'

'Thirty years,' said Jake. 'Give or take.'

Luke scowled and came in hard, peppering his brother with blows, his growing disillusion with Madeline

Delacourte giving him a ferocious edge. The fighting ceased being a sparring exercise and became instead an outlet for emotion of the explosive kind as he went for Jake's hands, the better to rid them of the long stick. Not a berserker, not quite, but a creature of instinct nonetheless and one Jake would have no peaceable defence against.

Cursing his lack of control, Luke grounded his staff and stepped back abruptly, breathing hard as he bowed to formalise the end of the session. 'Sorry,' he muttered, and headed for the stack of towels piled on a low wooden bench over by the wall.

Jake had walked towards Po and was speaking to him in the calm quiet way that Luke had always loved about his brother. The kid nodded once, warily, and hightailed it out of the dojo door. Jake turned his attention back to Luke after that. Luke looked away and towelled his face, not wanting to meet Jake's condemning gaze, or, worse, his understanding one. Once a younger brother, always a younger brother, though he was not the youngest of the four boys in the family. Tristan carried that dubious honour.

By the time he'd finished roughing the towel over his shoulders and stomach, Jake stood beside him.

'You want to tell me what that was all about?' asked Jake quietly.

Ten rigorous years of living life in the explosive lane? Never settling down, never staying in one place for more than a few months? One too many dices with death? A volcanic recklessness that had been building and building and needed an outlet before it blew him apart? 'I changed the rules on you halfway through the match and I shouldn't have. I stopped. No one got hurt. What's to tell?'

'You let anger take hold,' said Jake. 'You lost your centre.'

He didn't have a centre. He wasn't even sure he had a soul any more after standing witness to so much death and destruction. And the thought that Madeline Delacourte, saviour of street urchins, had sold her soul for wealth ate at him like acid. Just *once* he'd wanted an angel of mercy to grace his life rather than the spectre of death.

'How long since you last took a job?' Jake asked next.

'A few weeks back, give or take.' Not that he minded. Better for everyone when he wasn't working.

'You right for money?'

'Money's fine.' Luke's line of work had paid remarkably well over the years. He wasn't in Madeline Delacourte's stratosphere by any means, but he had no monetary need to ever work again.

Jake opened his mouth and closed it again without speaking. His face took on a pained expression. 'Blame your brothers,' he murmured.

'For what?'

'This. You're not in love, are you?'

Luke stared at him in astonishment. 'What?'

'No uncontrollable yearning to phone, visit, or possess one particular woman above all others?' Jake asked warily.

'No.' Not unless he counted wanting to possess the sister of mercy who'd just sashayed out of Jake's dojo without a backward glance. Which he didn't.

'This is a good thing,' said Jake. And with his next breath, 'So what the hell's your problem?'

'I don't know.' Something about this brother demanded honesty and always had. Luke gave it to him straight. 'It's just…walk in the shadow of violence long enough and it begins to claim you. I looked at Madeline Delacourte and saw beauty, not just of form but in deed as well. When your words painted her otherwise I saw red.'

Jake frowned as he towelled himself down. 'There's goodness in Maddy—ask any kid she's dragged from the gutter. There's beauty in the way she walks this city's dark side without fear. As for marrying to secure a better life—maybe she did, maybe she didn't—it's none of my business. And it doesn't make her a whore.'

Luke scowled. 'It doesn't exactly make her pure as the driven snow either.'

'What do you care? An angelic woman would drive you insane within a week.'

'Yes, but it'd be nice to know they *exist*.'

'When I find one I'll give you a call,' said Jake dryly. 'Meanwhile, I suggest you respect Madeline Delacourte for what she is. A smart and generous woman who doesn't give a damn if she has more enemies amongst the upper echelons of society than friends. She does what they don't. She pours truckloads of money into programmes designed to help the poor and displaced. She gets her hands dirty. And she doesn't judge people according to past actions and find them wanting, the way you've just done.'

Luke scowled afresh. 'Point taken.' If Jake was willing to defend her, then she must be all right. Not an angel, just a mere mortal like everyone else. Angels were for fairy tales. He tossed his towel down on the bench. 'I might stay on the floor a while.' Work the forms, push his body hard and maybe, just maybe, bury his recklessness and his wrongful snap judgements beneath exhaustion.

Jake slid him a sideways glance, cool and assessing. 'Fight me again,' he offered. 'Street rules, this time. No long sticks. No holding back. Just you and me.'

'What if I hurt you?' asked Luke gruffly, even as the beast within him roared its approval at Jake's offer.

'You won't.' Jake smiled gently. 'But feel free to try.'

Jake had given Luke unspoken permission to work off his anger and during the fighting that followed he did, sending more and more his brother's way until Jake faced the whole of it, drawing it from him effortlessly and shaping it into something harmless, something almost beautiful in its purity of intent. Fifteen minutes later, when they were both breathing hard and dripping sweat, Luke finally felt his tension start to ease.

Twenty minutes in, conspicuously on the losing end of this bout and grinning like a loon, Luke took the match to the floor and karate-with-intent turned to curse-and-laugh-filled wrestling. One last almighty elbow jab to Luke's solar plexus and Jake had him licked.

'You'd better be feeling better,' said Jake, wiping his mouth with the back of his hand as he staggered to his feet. 'Because I'm sure as hell feeling worse.'

Luke tried to sit up, groaned in pain, and thought the better of it. Flat on his back on the floor was just fine. Nice view of the ceiling from here. Jake's conquering grin came into view first, then his hand. Luke batted it away. 'Go away. I'm meditating.'

'You? Meditate?' Luke had never really mastered the finer points of meditation, and Jake knew it. 'On what?'

'Cobwebs. There's one in your light fitting.' Jake swore

blue that meditation was simply a variation on the absolute focus Luke brought to the dismantling of bombs. Trouble was, Luke couldn't bring that kind of focus to anything *but* unexploded weaponry. He certainly couldn't wish it into being while contemplating his navel, even if his navel *was* a metaphor for life, the universe, and everything.

'Cobweb meditation is good,' murmured Jake. 'Cobwebs can draw you to the centre of things and reveal hidden truths. Mind you, it'd help if you closed your eyes and stopped trying to incinerate your retinas while you're at it.'

'Always the perfectionist,' muttered Luke, but he closed his eyes and breathed deeply.

'What do you see?' asked Jake.

'The back of my eyelids.'

Jake sighed. 'Focus.'

'I know. I know. I'm on it,' said Luke. 'I'm moving my mind out into the flow.'

'Good. What do you see?'

The face of a woman, bright against the darkness. Shoulder-length honey-blonde hair styled straight with a full fringe. Moss-green eyes flecked with brown and framed by sable lashes. A wide mobile mouth made for laughter and kissing. She would kiss very well; he knew it instinctively. She could make a man believe there was good in the world.

Madeline Delacourte.

Luke snapped his eyes open and sat up fast, never mind the pain coursing through his side or the thorn of desire lodged deep in whatever passed these days for his soul.

'Anything?' asked Jake.

Luke shook his head. 'Nothing you want to know.'

CHAPTER TWO

MADELINE made a habit of following up on her re-homed street kids the day after she'd dropped them off at their new abode. Nimble-fingered Po had many survival strategies and scams in place, most of which would be calling for his attention right about now. If Jake could manage to keep Po around the dojo for the next forty-eight hours or so...if Jake could offer the boy something to work towards, something he wanted *more* than his old way of life...then Po had a chance at staying off the streets. That first step away from the old life was always the hardest, Maddy knew, but it could be done.

All Po needed was the right incentive.

Jacob was fronting a kick-boxing class when she walked into his dojo. He scowled when he saw her and jerked his head towards the back rooms, the half a dozen tiny rooms where guests and visiting students stayed, along with the occasional wayward boy.

She found Po in the kitchenette, kneeling on the round table, his attention firmly fixed on an odd assortment of kitchen appliances that had been placed dead centre of the round. Luke Bennett stood opposite Po, fully clothed this time, which was something of a disappointment, his voice a low rumble and his head bent as he too focused on the stuff on the table. Some sort of rolled-out cloth-bound toolkit lay between boy and man, only these particular tools weren't like any other implements Maddy had ever seen.

'Nearly done,' Luke's voice rolled over her, low and soothing. 'Steady. Steady. Just a li-i-ttle bit more. Okay, Po. *Now*.' Po's hands moved quick and sure as he wielded a tiny pair of wire cutters over a mass of wires, Luke's fingers just as nimble as he unwound a silver spring and shoved a piece of what looked like Blu-tack in its place. Moments later both boy and man leaned back, their grins wide and white. 'You've got good hands, kid. I'll give you that,' said Luke.

Po beamed. Maddy stared.

'Is that—' she couldn't believe her eyes '—a *bomb*?'

'Of course not. What kind of question is that?' Luke finally deemed fit to look her way, laughter lurking just around the corner. Maddy felt the force of that vivid amber gaze clear down to her toes. 'It's a makeshift detonation mechanism attached to a toaster.'

Maddy opened her mouth to speak but no words came out. Where to *begin*?

'Luke's got it set up to burn toast unless we can disable the detonator in time,' added Po.

'And the *wallet* in the toaster?' she asked acidly. 'What does that do?'

Po suddenly found the cracked linoleum floor pattern fascinating. Madeline stifled a groan. 'Po, who owns the wallet?'

'Jake,' said Luke. 'Po liberated it from him this morning and I liberated it from Po. Po's currently planning to put it back where he found it. He'd appreciate my silence on the issue. The main problem being that once I set the wallet to toasting, Po has approximately a minute to disable the detonator without jamming the toaster. Any longer than that and I'm pretty sure Jake's going to notice the scorch marks.'

Still nowhere to begin. Anywhere would do.

'Okay, debatable disciplinary measures aside, you don't think it slightly unwise to be teaching a *child* how to build and dismantle a trigger mechanism for a *bomb*?' She'd started the sentence with her voice low and controlled, the better to avoid shrieking by the time she got to the end.

'Maybe under ordinary circumstances, yes, but look at it this way,' said Luke, using that same soothing voice he'd used earlier. Unlike earlier, when she'd been reluctantly charmed, it made her want to strangle him. 'Po's a pickpocket. A career that values steady nerves and nimble hands is a natural progression for him.'

'Exactly *how*,' she said, with a generous dollop of sarcasm, 'is a career in bomb disposal *progression*?'

'Well, for one thing it's *legal*.'

'Did you mention how if you stuff up, you *die*?'

'Happens I did,' said Luke. 'I'm all for full disclosure.'

'There's so much to admire about you, Luke Bennett. Pity about the rest.'

'Oh, that's harsh,' he murmured without an ounce of repentance. 'Sorry, kid,' he said to Po. 'Lesson cancelled. I suggest you think hard about whether or not you're prepared to live by my brother's rules because I'm telling you now, you won't get a second chance with him. If it's easy money you're after, go back to picking pockets. Then when you grow up you can join the real thieves and be an investment banker.' Luke slid Maddy a sideways glance. 'Or you can always try the minimal-effort, time-honoured method of improving your lot in life and marry someone with money. Happens all the time.'

Maddy took the hit as she was meant to take it.

Personally.

'Now I know why your brother enjoys beating the daylights out of you,' she murmured.

'Trying,' corrected Luke helpfully. 'He enjoys *trying* to beat the daylights out of me. There's a difference.'

'Po, will you excuse us for a moment, please?' said Madeline.

'Can I get the wallet first?'

'Maybe later,' said Luke. 'And if you steal anything else of Jake's I swear you'll be cleaning the dojo floor with a toothbrush.'

Po grinned and disappeared.

'Is *your* room locked?' asked Madeline sweetly.

Luke cursed and headed for the door. 'Stay here,' he told her and pointed towards the table. 'Guard that while I escort Po to a kick-boxing class.'

'Ah, the masculine mind at work,' murmured Maddy as he swept past her, all hard and determined male. 'It's a wondrous thing.'

'It'd help a lot if you didn't actually *speak*,' he said.

She blew him a kiss instead. 'Is that better?'

'No.'

She smiled her commiseration.

Only when she was sure Luke Bennett was out of sight did Madeline give in to curiosity and turn her attention to the device on the table. Five minutes later she thought she had the simplicities of the detonation mechanism figured.

'You should ask for permission before you start playing with a man's toys,' said a chocolate-smooth voice from behind her. 'They might not be harmless.'

Luke. He of the steady hands, stupendous body, and small brain.

'What would happen if I cut this wire here?' she asked.

'Nothing.'

'What about this one?'

'Cut that one and life gets interesting,' he said. 'Jake said you and he were just friends.'

'Aw-w-w. You're still concerned about poaching? Aren't you sweet?' Best to turn and face danger head on—the better to know when to run. Madeline hadn't learned that in any fancy Swiss finishing school but the lesson had stood her in excellent stead over the years nonetheless. She braced herself as she turned her head to look at him in an attempt to lessen the impact of that clear golden gaze. 'But Jake's right. I consider him a friend. I'm glad to hear that he considers me one.'

'You didn't know that he thinks of you as a friend?' asked Luke with the lift of an eyebrow.

'Your brother's not an easy man to read,' she offered with a slight smile. Madeline pitied the woman who set her sights on Jacob Bennett, she really did. 'He doles his smiles and his welcomes out sparingly. You, on the other hand, don't.'

'Is this a bad thing?' The smile Luke bestowed on her held more than its share of wicked charm.

'For you? No.' For the women on the receiving end of those easy smiles, she thought it might be. Time to stop gazing at that arresting face and concentrate on something else, decided Madeline. Like the stretch of a grey T-shirt over a chest wide and muscled. Like the play of veins from his elbows to his wrists as he leaned in beside her, his forearms on the table and his attention on the toaster.

Luke's shoulder brushed hers, ever so briefly, and ever so deliberately. No way did this man not know where every millimetre of his was at any given time. He turned his head towards her and his gaze skated over her face and came to rest on her mouth with a focus that made Madeline's breath hitch somewhere in her throat and stay there.

Madeline's gaze slid helplessly to the sensual curve of *his* lips. Passion abundant, yet underscored by a firmness that hinted at iron control when Luke wanted control. Laughter in the grooves around the edges of those lips.

'Seen enough?' he murmured, and she who never blushed felt warmth creep up her neck and along her cheeks.

'I think so.' Cursing his appeal and her blatant reaction to it, Madeline turned her attention back to the apparatus on the table. 'Where were we?'

'No idea,' he said. 'But I think we should get it over with. It'd speed things up and, seeing as I'm only here for a week…'

'Get what over with?'

'Our first kiss.' They were side by side, shoulder to shoulder, as he picked up the tiny wire cutters and carefully turned the detonator over to reveal another half a dozen wires. 'One of them will disable the detonator without jamming the toaster. Question is, which one?'

'I don't know.'

'You want to hazard a guess?'

'Not particularly,' she said. 'I like to know what I'm doing—and why—before I do it. Take kissing you, for example.'

'Good example,' he said.

'Happens I do know my way around a man's mouth,' she murmured. 'Thing is, I'm not altogether sure *why* I'd want to kiss a man who despises me.' She needed to see his face for this next question. She needed to think she wouldn't get lost when she looked his way. 'Is it the money you despise or the way I acquired it?'

'Maybe you didn't marry for money,' he said, his eyes not leaving her face as he threw down his own question. 'Maybe you loved your late husband.'

Maddy stared into those warm tiger eyes for a very long time, wishing her answer could have been different. Wishing she could have said yes, yes, she had. But the one thing Madeline had never been was a liar and she didn't intend to start now, no matter how strong the temptation. 'I married William Delacourte for security and for the lifestyle he could give me. He was a good man. I respected him and never cheated on him. But if you're asking me whether I loved him when I married him the answer is no.'

Luke Bennett didn't like that answer. She could see questions in his eyes—so many questions she didn't know how to answer—and behind the questions, condemnation.

'Did you sleep with him?' he asked.

'Have *you* been in love with every woman you've ever slept with?' she answered coolly.

'No,' he answered, equally cool. 'Did he know you didn't love him?'

'Yes.'

'Poor bastard,' murmured Luke. But he didn't move away, and neither did she.

'Any more questions?' she said.

'Yeah.' Luke's lips twisted into a wry smile as his eyes grew intent. He still had his elbows resting on the Formica table. So did Madeline. But their faces were close, close enough that it would only take the tilt of her head and a slight forward movement to make their mouths meet. 'Are you sure you don't want that kiss?'

'Now why would I want to kiss you,' she murmured, 'when you don't even like me?'

'Beats me,' he said. 'Do it anyway.'

He had the knack of making Maddy want things she shouldn't. Like lips against hers, firm and knowing. Like being cradled in the arms of a warrior who could make her see only the moment, and to hell with the life choices that surrounded it. How *did* one approach desire when they weren't intending to exploit it? Maddy didn't know.

She wanted to know.

With her elbows still firmly resting on the table, Madeline eased closer and set her mouth to Luke's.

She didn't rush to taste him, content for the moment with the feel of firm lips barely touching hers. Such fleeting contact. So blindingly perfect. Luke's scent wrapped around her and the heat in him shuddered through her as she closed her eyes and touched the tip of her tongue to that firm upper lip the better to taste him.

He didn't rush her. He simply let her play at exploring his lips, the shape and texture of them. A man of patience and timing, Luke Bennett, as finally, when she was just about to pull back, he turned his body towards her, and opened the way to deeper exploration. The slide of his tongue against hers, savouring and sensual. The hitch of his breath as she savoured him in turn. Then a ragged curse as his hand came up to sink into her hair and cradle the back of her head as he deepened the kiss.

Focused, so utterly focused on the moment and on her. Reckless with what he gave away. Passion to savour, passion to burn, as reality faded away beneath the radiance of this man making love to her mouth.

'How old were you?' Luke murmured as his lips finally left hers, rendering her bereft and craving more of him. More kisses, more contact, more pleasure. 'How old were you when you married him, Maddy? Did you even *know* what you were giving up?'

'Old enough.' She kissed him one last time, slow and deep, craving oblivion. Wishing she could be what this man so obviously wanted her to be. Young. Naive. Innocent. But she'd never been any of those things, she'd never had the luxury, and he needed to know and accept that.

If he could.

Slowly, reluctantly, Madeline pulled out of the kiss and put some distance between them. The table for starters. And then the truth. 'And, yes, I knew full well what I was doing when I forfeited love and passion for wealth and security. I've never regretted paying the price.

I wish…' How she wished she could have brought a bright and shiny past to this man's table. But she couldn't. Pointless to wish that things could have been different. 'Never mind.'

Madeline watched in silence as Luke cursed and turned away.

'I can't,' he said, and shook his head as if to clear it. 'I don't…'

'Don't what? Don't even like me?' She tried to make light of it. 'I get that a lot.'

'*Don't* put words in my mouth.' He sent her a searing golden glare. 'I like you plenty.'

'Maybe. But you wish to hell you didn't,' she added, and her smile was one she'd perfected over the years, cool and mocking, mocking them both. 'I get that a lot too.'

CHAPTER THREE

LUKE didn't try to argue against her second statement, and Maddy gave him points for honesty. She gave him more points for staying right where he was as he fought to bring the rawness of their encounter back into line with what was civilised and polite and socially acceptable.

'Here's the thing, Luke Bennett,' she said softly. 'You think you know what I am. Well, I know what you are, too. An adrenalin junkie; a man who's come to terms with an early death in the service of others because what else is there? It's in your eyes, in the way you move. You don't care for life and you know nothing of love. It's never claimed you. You ask for a kiss but you'd take a heart and never even notice what you'd done. So don't you judge me, Luke Bennett, and I won't judge you.'

That was twice now in as many days that Luke had been called to task for errors in judgement. He was trying to give Madeline the benefit of the doubt, heaven help him he *was* trying, but every time he thought he had a handle on her she showed him otherwise.

The information on Madeline Delacourte wasn't all bad, certainly. There was his attraction to her—surely that had to count for something, for he wasn't usually prone to wanting hard-hearted women. Easy-going and light on commitment, yes. Heartless, no. That Jake valued Madeline's friendship counted for more. And then there was this huge gaping hole in Madeline's conscience when it came to marrying for wealth, and *that* was the bit he couldn't stomach.

'Are we interrupting?' said a voice from the doorway, and, with serious effort required on his part, Luke broke free of Maddy's shuttered gaze and looked towards his brother. Jake stood there scowling at him and he wasn't alone. Po stood beside Jake, his scowl equally well presented. 'Because we can come back later,' said Jake, heavy on the sarcasm.

'We should stay,' said Po to Jake in rapid Mandarin that Luke could only just follow. 'If we go they'll probably kill each other or something.'

'I get that feeling too,' said Jake.

'Nice to see the two of you bonding so fast,' said Madeline. 'And just for the record, I wouldn't have killed him.'

'I probably wouldn't have killed her either,' muttered Luke.

'The week is still young,' said Jake dryly. 'I recommend distance and denial, but since when has anyone ever listened to me? As for Po here, we've yet to decide if his staying on is an arrangement that will suit us. Come back tomorrow.'

'Tomorrow's not good for me,' said Madeline with a careless shrug. 'It's a distance and denial thing.'

'Don't mind me,' said Luke. If Madeline could pull back from the earth-shattering kiss they'd just shared and

put the carnage that had followed behind her, then so
could he. 'I won't be around. Things to do.'

'So that's settled, then?' Jacob's gaze cut to Maddy.
'Come by around midday and we'll feed you.'

For some obscure reason that Luke really didn't want
to think about, tomorrow's happy-family scenario didn't
sit well with him. He didn't look at Madeline and he sure
as hell didn't look at Jake as he shouldered roughly past
him and stepped out into the corridor. It wasn't until
Luke hit the street that he realised he had company. Po
skipped alongside him, keeping up but only just. Mind-
ing his distance, but only so much. Luke stopped. So did
Po, hanging back. Not afraid of him—at least Luke
hoped he wasn't—just cautious in the way of all half-
wild things.

'Did Jake get you to follow me?'

Po shot Luke a wary glance. 'No.'

'Then why are you here?'

'I wanted out too. Needed to walk. Go get some stuff.'

'What kind of stuff?'

'My stuff.'

'Stolen?'

Po just looked at him.

Time to rephrase. 'Stuff that'll get you jailed if you're
caught with it?'

'No. Some clothes, some Sing.' Sing being Singapore
dollars. 'I won't bring anything else.'

Luke really didn't want to know what else the kid had
that he wouldn't be bringing. 'Where do you have to go?'

'Bugis Street.'

In years gone by, Old Bugis Street had been the traditional home of every vice known to man and then some. Redevelopment had sanitised the area but, like rats in a city sewer, you could never silence sin. 'Maddy said you worked Orchid Road.'

'Yeah, but I live on Bugis Street.'

Live. Not lived. Luke didn't like the present-tense inference. 'You know, kid? Po? If you're even half serious about making a fresh start, going back to Bugis Street won't help.'

Po just looked at him. Dark eyes in a pinched face and a body that was decades too small for the soul that resided within.

Luke didn't want to get involved—he was only in Singapore for the week. But, 'You need some company?' was what he said.

'Do you?' said the boy, and fell into step beside him.

A couple of blocks went by in silence. Po clearly didn't see the need for conversation. 'How did you meet Madeline?' Luke finally asked the kid.

'She looked rich,' said Po. 'Her handbag was Prada and her shoes were Chanel—the real deal. So I marked her.'

'You *stole* from her?'

'Tried to,' said Po. 'But she knew all the moves. It was like she could see inside me. She asked me if I was hungry. When I said yes, she took me to a street stall and she knew the owner. She gave him five hundred Sing and told him to feed me for a month. He did.'

'Did you stop picking pockets after that?'

'I stopped trying to pick *her* pocket after that,' said Po piously. 'She'd come to the street stall every Monday. I used to sit with her sometimes.'

'And after your month of free meals was up?'

'It was never up. Grandfather Cheung said she'd paid for another month and that I could hang around in the shop overnight so long as I helped him get the shopfront ready for business the next morning. He has three grandsons but they don't move fast. I do.'

'Sounds like a sweet deal,' said Luke. For a homeless child thief. 'What went sour?'

'Old man Cheung got sick and sold the shop. A couple of weeks later a street boss offered me a job I didn't want to take. Maddy said it was time for me to move on and that she knew of a place.'

'You trusted her?'

'She said there was this sensei who took students and he was like this warrior monk or something. She said we could walk there and that I could leave any time.'

A monk, eh? Luke shook his head. Maybe there were some similarities between Jake's dedication to martial arts and the celestial path a spiritual man might walk, but Jake a monk? Hardly. 'So Jake takes you in on Madeline's say-so, gives you food and a room and you steal his wallet? Where's the sense in that?'

'I wasn't going to *steal* anything from his wallet. I just wanted to know what was in it.'

'Why?'

'So I could find out more about the sensei.'

'How?'

'From his cards and his receipts. From driver's licence and the picture he keeps behind it.'

'Jake keeps a picture behind his driver's licence?'

'Of a woman,' said Po. 'Could be Singlish. Chinese hair, western eyes.'

'Ji,' said Luke curtly. 'Jake's ex.'

'Ex what?'

'Wife.'

'Monks have wives?' said Po.

'No.' Jake didn't deserve the responsibility that went with having a curious child thrust upon him, thought Luke grimly. He really didn't.

It took them twenty minutes to get to where Po wanted to go, a set of garbage bins in an alleyway beside an all-night noodle bar. There was a drainage grate set into the wall behind the bins, big enough for a hand and elbow, but not a boy. Hell of a moneybox.

'Can you keep watch?' asked Po as he slipped behind the bins.

Curiosity over what might lie behind the grate warred with Luke's need to protect the boy and his doings from the eyes of others. Every kid had a cupboard, he tried to reassure himself. This was Po's. No need to know what else was in it apart from clothes and the money the boy wanted to retrieve. Trust was a two-way street and had to start somewhere, right?

Madeline had seen something in the boy worth rescuing.

Jake had trusted Madeline's judgement enough to take Po in.

Judgement.

Madeline.

Po and his cupboard.

Cursing himself for a fool, Luke strode back to where the alleyway met the street and leaned against the wall, a bystander or a player, it didn't matter. Just another tourist watching the show.

Ahead of him lay five more days in the vicinity of Madeline Delacourte.

Behind him lay a tiny thief with his hand up a drain.

Madeline didn't linger long in Jacob's presence after Luke and Po had disappeared. Long enough for a question or two from Jacob that she hadn't wanted to answer, that was all.

'You want to talk about what you're doing to my brother, Maddy?'

'No.' Talk was overrated.

'Do you need me to tell you that if you play him, and hurt him, we may not be able to remain friends?'

'No.' She already had that bit figured. She'd had a younger brother too. Once. She picked up her handbag. Jacob stood aside to let her pass. 'I know the thickness of blood,' she said quietly. And the fragility of friendship. 'I wasn't playing your brother for sport, Jacob. I wasn't playing him at all.'

She didn't know why she'd done what she'd done with Luke Bennett.

'Maddy…' Jacob's gruff voice stopped her in the doorway. 'Even if you're not playing with him…don't hurt him.'

Madeline smiled faintly. 'You care about him a lot, don't you?'

'He's my brother.' Jacob ran his hand through already untidy hair. 'I care for you too. As a friend, you understand. Not as a…' Jacob appeared to be at a loss for words. 'You know.'

'I understand.'

'Good,' he said awkwardly. 'Because I don't want you getting hurt either.'

'I understand.'

'Good,' he said again. 'So that's settled, then?'

'Definitely.'

'See you tomorrow.'

'Can't wait.'

Madeline stepped out of the dojo, hailed a taxi, and headed for the nearest gin and tonic, silently rueing the day she met her first Bennett brother and thanking her lucky stars there'd been a ten-year interim in which to get used to the breed before she'd met her second.

Jake took one look at his wallet sitting in the toaster and headed for the Scotch.

CHAPTER FOUR

MADELINE kept her lunch appointment with Jacob and Po the following day, never mind that staying away from the dojo while Luke was in residence seemed by far the better option. She had a burning need to help the runaways of the world find their way home, and if that wasn't possible then she would find them a place where they could flourish and grow as children should grow. Strange as it seemed, Jacob's dojo was such a haven.

Half-grown outcasts felt comfortable there. *Madeline* felt comfortable there, never mind that martial arts could be a brutal sport and Jacob had no mind to soften it. The dojo rules were fair and clear and utterly unbreakable.

If Po could abide by such rules, Jacob would see to it that the kid thrived.

Jacob and Po were working behind the counter today, Jacob on the computer with Po standing at his shoulder, watching intently.

'He can't read,' said Jacob when he saw her. 'He needs to be in school.'

'No family information that Po's willing to share with me, a fierce aversion to being logged into the system, no school,' said Madeline in reply. 'I figured housing came first and school could come later.'

'A tutor, then,' said Jacob.

'That I can arrange.' Madeline looked around casually. No Luke.

'He's not here,' said Jacob without looking up from the screen.

'Did I *ask*?' said Madeline.

'No, but you wanted to,' said Jacob. Boy and man swapped amused glances.

So they were right. Madeline shot them a narrowed glare. That didn't mean she had to admit they were right. 'Yesterday, you mentioned lunch,' she said. 'I've got twenty minutes.'

'Why so tight?' asked Jacob. 'Problems with the empire?'

'Always.' She'd inherited a crumbling empire, not a thriving one. Staying one step ahead of the creditors had taken ingenuity and time. Fortunately, she'd had plenty of both. Madeline could play the widowed trophy wife to perfection when it suited her, but anyone doing business with Delacourte knew differently. The Delacourte upstart didn't leech off Delacourte enterprises, she *ran* them, along with a fair few charity institutions on the side. 'A meeting with the accountant beckons.'

'I've got leftover *mee goreng*, a microwave, and an apprentice who knows his way around a kitchen,' said Jacob.

'You want me to fix the food?' said Po.

Jacob nodded and the boy slipped away, swift and silent.

'Has he taken to karate?' she asked.

Jacob nodded, eyeing her tailored black business suit

with a frown. 'Po moves fast, thinks fast, and he's so used to living rough that anything I set him to do is a softness. He and Luke started on some karate forms at around midnight last night and finished around two a.m. He was up again at six. The kid'll nap now in snatches throughout the day and snap awake the moment something moves, ready to either fight or run. Breaks your heart.'

'He'll settle, though, won't he? Eventually?'

'Maybe.' Jacob ran a hand through his hair. 'I don't know. Luke's got a better handle on him than I do. Maybe you should talk to Luke.'

Not quite what she had in mind. 'Why? What does he say?'

'He says he'll stay another week unless a job comes up. And that he'll keep an eye on Po while he's here.'

'And your brother can just do that? Change his plans on a whim?'

'The man's a free agent, Maddy. Would you think more of him if he *couldn't* stay and help out for a while?'

'I'm trying not to think of him at all,' she muttered.

'Is it working?' said a silken voice from behind her. Madeline knew it was Luke, even before she turned to face him. Her body's response to his nearness was very thorough.

He wore a faded grey T-shirt, loose-fitting jeans, and a look in his eye that told her that if she had any sense she'd turn and run and keep right on running. 'Where's Po?' he said.

'Kitchen,' replied Jacob.

With a curt nod in Madeline's direction, Luke left. Madeline made a concerted effort not to watch him go.

Jacob just looked at her and sighed.

'What?' she said defiantly.

'Nothing,' said Jacob. 'Nothing I want to talk about at any rate.'

Amen.

Luke made himself conspicuously absent during lunch. Po showed Madeline the room Jake had given him afterwards—bare walls, bare bulb, a chest of drawers, a bed, white sheets and a thin grey coverlet. Jacob was a minimalist when it came to possessions but Po seemed overwhelmed by the space and the fixtures that had suddenly been deemed his. Madeline asked Po if he felt like staying on as Jacob's apprentice. If she'd done the right thing in bringing him here.

Po nodded jerkily. Yes.

She'd seen a noodle bar across the street from the dojo that she thought she might try out next Monday lunchtime. She could use some company if Po felt inclined to stop by…

Another nod. System sorted.

Madeline left the dojo with five minutes to spare before the start of her next meeting. It would take her another ten minutes to get to the accounting firm's offices so she was already running late, even before she spotted Luke Bennett leaning against a shopfront wall not two doors down from the dojo, idly seeming to watch the world go by.

While waiting for her to leave.

She walked towards him slowly, stopped in front of him. Neither of them spoke. But he looked at her and in that fierce heated glance lay a dialogue as old as time.

'I wanted you to look this way and walk the other,' he

said finally. Had she been listening to his words alone she might have kept on walking, but those eyes and the tension in that hard, lean body of his told a different story.

'No, you didn't.'

'I dreamed of you last night,' he said next. Not the sweet murmurings of a soon-to-be lover, but cold, hard accusation.

'Snap.' She'd dreamed of him too, her sleeping time shattered by a golden-eyed warrior whose righteousness cut at her even as his kisses seduced. 'Jacob said you and Po trained for half the night.'

'We did.' No need to guess *why* he'd chosen physical exertion over dreaming. He hadn't wanted to dream of her. He couldn't have said it any plainer. 'I still think walking away from you is the smart option,' he murmured.

'Then do it.'

He glanced away, looked down the street as if planning where he would walk, but his body stayed right where it was. When he looked back at her the reckless challenge in his eyes burned a path through every defence she had in place. 'No.'

Oh, boy.

'Come out with me tonight,' he said next.

'Where?' Was asking about a venue a tacit agreement? She thought it might be.

'Anywhere,' he muttered. 'Do I look like I care?'

A shudder ripped through Madeline, two parts desire and one part dread for the wanton images that played out in her mind every time she looked at this man.

Luke's eyes darkened. 'You choose,' he said. 'Maybe you'll care.' Somewhere with people, if she had any sense

at all. Somewhere crowded and casual. There were plenty
such places in Singapore. She could easily suggest she
meet him at one of them.

She didn't.

Instead, she gave him her home address. 'I'll try and
book us a table somewhere. I'll be home by six. Ready
to head out again by seven.'

He nodded, shoved his hands in his pockets and leaned
his head back against the wall, everything about him
casual except for his eyes. There was nothing casual
about them at all. 'You should go now,' he said.

Madeline nodded and forced a step back before she
did something monumentally stupid like setting her
hands to his chest and her lips to his throat and to hell
with empires and accountants. 'Jacob knows my mobile
number.' Luke's eyes narrowed, as if he either didn't like
that notion or he didn't know where she was heading with
this. 'Call me if you decide to cancel.'

'Do you really think I will?'

'No.' She offered up a tiny smile of farewell. 'But I'm
fairly certain you should.'

Madeline made it home just on six-thirty but instead of
the fatigue that usually accompanied an afternoon spent
wading through financial statements, nervous anticipation ruled her now. She didn't make a habit of handing
over her home address to men she'd just met. Even if
Luke was Jake's brother there'd been no call for that. But
she had, and she'd wear it. Wear something. What on
earth was she going to wear this evening?

A wizened old woman appeared in the foyer, her face

leathered and lined but her old eyes clear and smiling. Yun had been William's housekeeper for at least thirty years, maybe longer. Now she was Madeline's and more grand-mother than housekeeper if truth were told.

'We've company coming at seven,' said Madeline as she shed her light coat and slid a wall panel aside to reveal a cleverly concealed wardrobe. 'Can we do some kind of canapés?'

'What kind of company?' asked Yun.

'Male.'

'How many?'

'One.'

'Nationality?'

'Australian.'

'Age?' Yun could put foreign embassy officials to shame when it came to tailoring hospitality to fit circumstance.

'My age.'

Yun's immaculately pencilled eyebrows rose. 'A business associate?'

'No. Jacob Bennett's brother. He's taking me out to dinner.'

'Where?'

Good question, for she'd yet to make a reservation. 'I thought maybe somewhere touristy, down by the water.' If they went to the wharves they wouldn't even have to book in advance. They could just choose a place as they wandered along.

Yun's eyes narrowed to slits. 'Does he not know how to properly honour a woman of your social standing?'

Madeline stifled a grin. 'You'd rather he took me somewhere intimate and expensive?'

'Just expensive,' said Yun.

'I don't think he's the kind of man who cares much for the trappings of wealth or for impressing a woman with fine food and wine.'

'Really?' Yun seemed unimpressed. 'What kind of man is he?'

'Well…' Apart from the kind who could make a woman abandon every ounce of common sense she'd ever had? 'I don't rightly know.'

'When was he born? What's his animal?'

'I don't know.' Yun was old school. She practised feng shui, observed the Chinese zodiac, and honoured her ancestor spirits. 'I'm going to go with Tiger.'

'Tiger is unpredictable,' murmured Yun. 'And dangerous. Tiger and Snake not good together. Each can destroy the other if allowed to get too close.'

'Thanks, Yun. I feel so much better now.' Madeline had been born in the year of the snake. Nice to know in advance how incompatible she and Luke truly were.

'Monkey is better fit for you. Even Ox. Find out his birth year.'

'Will do. So can you do up a tray of something?'

'Of course,' said Yun. 'Something for harmony and relaxation.'

'Perfect.' Madeline could use some harmony and relaxation, what with her incompatible love life and all. She started across the high-gloss white marble floor, only to whirl back around with a new question. 'What should I wear?'

'A dress shaped for beauty, a smile for serenity, and your antique jade hairpin,' said Yun. 'For luck.'

* * *

Luke Bennett was a punctual man, discovered Madeline as the state-of-the-art security cameras showed him summoning the private lift to the apartment block's foyer area at five minutes to seven that evening. Madeline had taken Yun's advice and wore a fitted deep-green dress that emphasised her assets and the green flecks in her eyes. Yun had helped wind her hair up into an elegant roll, secured with many hidden pins. The jade hairpin came last—with its five silver threads studded with tiny oyster pearls.

'Stop fidgeting,' said Yun, and prepared to open the door. 'He's just a man.'

'Right.' Just a man.

A man who wore dark grey dress trousers and a crisp white shirt with an ease she'd never expected of him. A man whose elegant clothes served only to emphasise the raw power and masculinity of the body beneath. His dark hair was tousled and his face could have launched a thousand fantasies and probably had. It was the eyes that did it—those magnificent tawny eyes.

'You're no Monkey,' said Yun accusingly. 'And you definitely no Ox.'

Luke Bennett stared down at the tiny woman whose head barely topped his elbow. 'No,' he said as his bemused and oddly helpless gaze cut to Madeline. 'I'm not.'

A helpless Luke Bennett settled Madeline's butterflies considerably. 'Yun, this is Luke Bennett. Luke, meet Yun, my housekeeper.'

'Could be Dragon but not so likely.' Yun sighed sorrowfully. 'I'll bring out the antelope.'

Not a lot a man could say to a statement like that. Luke said nothing, just watched Yun disappear through

a wide archway as she headed for the kitchen.
Madeline summoned a hostess's smile as Luke returned
his gaze to her, seemingly oblivious to the wall full of
museum-quality silk tapestries and the occasional
priceless vase.

'How's Po?' she asked.

'Busy, I hope. Because when he's not he's prodi-
giously good at finding trouble.'

'And your brother?'

'Also busy.'

And that was the extent of Madeline's small talk.
Common ground extinguished. Dangerous new territory
stretching out before them. She wondered if Luke knew
what he was doing in pursuing the lightning attraction
that sparked between them. Madeline certainly didn't.

She'd always preferred *not* to play with lightning.

'Would you like a drink?' Madeline moved towards a
high-topped bench in the corner. The bar was behind it,
cleverly concealed by panelling that slid aside to reveal
the drinks selection on hand. Hospitality was important
in this part of the world and the subtleties of what was
offered and how were endless. William had taught her
that. Pity he hadn't taught her what to offer a golden-eyed
warrior who didn't necessarily like her but who wanted
her with an intensity that left her breathless. 'Yun's just
gone to get a tray of nibbles for us.'

'You didn't have to go to any trouble,' he murmured.

'It wasn't any trouble. Yun enjoys putting her culinary
talents to use.' Madeline offered up what she hoped was
a serene smile. 'She's done every cooking course known

to man, and she'll scold me if I haven't poured you a glass of something before she gets back.'

'With the antelope.'

'Let's hope not.' Madeline opened the bar fridge and peered at the contents. 'What would you like?'

'Just a beer.'

Madeline pulled a bottle of Tiger Bitter from the shelf and reached for the bottle opener. Pointless asking what year Luke had been born, really. His zodiac sign was a foregone conclusion. She retrieved a cold beer glass from the fridge and poured for him, before starting in on the fixings for a gin and tonic for herself. Staple fare in this part of the world—any time and anywhere.

'So what brought you to Singapore?' asked Luke as she found a lime and sliced into it with a paring knife. A quarter for his beer if he wanted one. Definitely a slice for her gin. And running alongside the busywork, small talk between strangers that should have been easy enough to answer but wasn't.

'I came here looking for my brother,' she said finally. 'He was travelling around South East Asia. Singapore had been his starting point, so it became mine as well.'

'Did you find him?'

'Eventually.' Madeline had no inclination to explain her extended crawl through the dark belly of humanity in search of Remy. 'He's dead now.' There'd been no saving him.

'I'm sorry.' Luke's clear gaze rested thoughtfully on her. 'Is that why you try and help children like Po?'

'Maybe.' Madeline shrugged. 'Probably. I saw a lot of things in my search for my brother—a lot of things I would fix if I could.'

'Is that why you married money? So you could fix the things you'd seen?'

'Still judging me, Luke Bennett?' Always, he seemed to circle back to the question of why she had married William.

'No.' And with a wry smile, 'Maybe. Maybe I'm just trying to get to know you a little better.'

Maybe she could give him the benefit of the doubt. 'My brother and I were orphans,' she told him. 'Wards of the State of New South Wales. Remy craved oblivion and found it. I craved security, stability, and wealth.'

'And found it,' said Luke.

Madeline nodded. 'Yes. Does knowing my background make my choice of marriage partner any more palatable to you?'

'I don't know.' Luke smiled bleakly and looked around the room.

Madeline looked too, trying to see her home through his eyes. An eclectic mix of the comfortable, the best, and a smattering of old and distinguished money in the form of sculptures and paintings. Madeline didn't deliberately flaunt the Delacourte wealth at her disposal, but she did enjoy it. No apologies.

'Nice place,' he said.

'Thank you.' She studied him a while longer. 'Money doesn't mean much to you, does it?'

He shrugged. 'I have enough. I've no need for more.' His eyes grew dark as his gaze met hers. 'You going to judge me wanting again, Maddy?'

'Because you don't crave wealth?' she said lightly. 'No. Each to their own.'

So different, she and Luke Bennett. Maybe even too

different. The man was reckless, where Madeline craved control. Addicted to danger, whereas she was addicted to security. As for him being unaware of the impact he had on a woman when he exploded into her life…she hadn't quite decided if he knew how truly potent he was or not. But judge him wanting? That she could not do. 'We really don't have much in common, do we?' she said.

'Not so far.' Luke put his drink down carefully on the coaster she'd provided. He leaned forward, elbows on the bar, closer, and closer still, until his lips were almost upon hers. 'But we might dig up something eventually,' he murmured, and Madeline's gaze dropped helplessly to his lips. 'That's what first dates are for.'

'And second kisses?' she whispered. 'What are they for?'

'They're to see if we remembered the first kiss wrong.' His lips brushed hers, slow and savouring before returning to offer up just that little bit more. Desire unfurled deep within her. She hadn't remembered their first kiss wrong.

He pulled back slowly and drew his bottom lip into his mouth as if committing the taste of her to memory.

'What are your feelings on standardising and enforcing international deep-sea-fishing quotas?' he murmured.

'I'm all for it,' she said. 'Although the enforcement bit could prove tricky.'

'I agree,' he said. 'Common ground at last.'

Not to mention uncommon heat in their kisses.

Yun chose that moment to enter the room with a tray of bite-sized spring rolls and a chilli dip. Smiling wryly, Madeline pulled back and turned her attention to the diminutive housekeeper.

'It's plenty hot,' warned Yun, with a sour sideways glance in Luke's direction. 'Fire is useful weapon against hunting Tiger. Bullets also,' she muttered, and disappeared.

'She's very loyal,' said Madeline.

'Not quite the word I had in mind,' murmured Luke, eyeing the finger food cautiously.

Madeline picked up a roll, dipped it into the dressing, popped it into her mouth and bit down through the flaky pastry to the mince mix beyond. So far, divine. But the bite of chilli was there, and growing ever stronger. It stopped short of a conflagration, but only just. 'They're very exciting,' she said hoarsely. 'You'll probably enjoy them.'

'What about the ones with the little squiggle on the side?' asked Luke.

Not a squiggle, thought Madeline, looking closely at the spring rolls, but a snake. 'Those are for me.'

He took one of those, dipped it in the sauce and made short work of it thereafter. 'They're good,' he said, reaching for another, this time without the snake motif on the side. This one made him smile. 'They're very good.'

'We should probably go soon,' she offered weakly. She didn't know what embarrassed her more: Yun's dubious hospitality or her body's extravagantly sensuous response to his recklessness. 'I haven't booked. I thought we might wander down towards—'

'The wharves,' he said.

'Exactly.' Plenty of water down by the wharves. She could use it to douse the flames.

The rows of restaurants surrounding the wharves shone crowded and cheerful, even if the food was hit and miss.

Lights from the surrounding city shimmered in the background and found reflection in the inky harbour water.

Luke sat back in his chair once they'd ordered their meals and aimed for casual conversation, the kind a man might make in passing. Did Madeline enjoy living in Singapore? Yes, she did. Had she ever considered heading home to Australia? No, she hadn't.

And then Madeline began to counter with questions of her own. Where was he based?

Nowhere of late, though he had an apartment in Darwin that he often returned to in between jobs. He didn't need much. He didn't *have* much.

Unlike some. She'd said that his lack of monetary focus didn't bother her and heaven help him he believed her. The problem now lay in deciding if the disparity in their wealth was going to eat at *him*. When it came to a short-term relationship, the extent of Madeline's wealth shouldn't bother him at all. It was only when he started thinking long term that her wealth and his comparative lack of it became an issue.

'What?' she asked, more attuned to him than he wanted her to be.

'What would you do if you woke up tomorrow and you'd lost all that Delacourte money your late husband left you?' Not that he *was* thinking long term. No way.

'Start again.'

'Beginning with marriage to a rich man?'

'Not necessarily,' she said with a shrug. 'I know a little something about the making and keeping of money these days. I'd probably try and make my own way.'

'You'd fight to be wealthy again?'

Her eyes flashed green fire. 'The Delacourte empire wasn't in particularly good shape when William died. I sold the family estate, bought the apartment I live in now, and used the change to restructure the company. Big business can mean big losses. I fight to stay wealthy *now*.'

'You like it,' he said. 'The fight.'

'So do you,' she countered. 'When it comes to your work you're all about challenge and danger and pitting yourself against the odds. Of course, when it comes to women, I've a very strong feeling that you're not looking for a fight at all. You're looking for perfection.' She leaned forward, her eyes warm and ever so slightly mocking. 'Sorry to disappoint.'

'You don't have to keep pointing out your flaws, Maddy. I can see them.'

She laughed at that, a rich vibrant chuckle that warmed an already sultry night.

'How exactly did you end up doing what you do?' she asked him, directing the conversation away from money and the making of it and back towards him. 'I can't imagine a school counsellor sitting you down to do a jobs test and saying that he thought you should diffuse bombs for a living.'

'He didn't. Though he did think a stint in the armed forces might not be such a bad thing should I ever wish to acquire some discipline. No, I followed my brother Pete into the Navy straight from school. Pete had his eyes on the sky, the Navy Seahawks. All I wanted to do was dive. After the training came the jobs, one of which was clearing sea mines. Then came retrieval of unexploded weaponry from various naval training grounds and I ended up as part of a three-man Explosive Ordnance Disposal Unit. Then some land-based work happened my way and I finished up with the Navy and went free-lance. I still consult for them every now and again. I teach for them too, on occasion.'

Madeline smiled wryly. 'Okay. I'll admit it. I'm impressed,' she said, and looked up as an immaculately dressed elderly Asian man paused on his way past their table. The rest of the man's party moved on ahead.

'Mr Yi,' said Madeline, not quite concealing her surprise, though she made a creditable attempt at a polite smile.

'Mrs Delacourte.' The briefest of bows accompanied the statement, before the man's gaze cut to Luke.

'May I introduce Luke Bennett, my dining companion?' said Madeline, responding to the unspoken cue, again with manners and caution rather than warmth. 'Luke, may I present to you Bruce Yi, philanthropist and financier.'

Luke stood and shook hands with the man. Firm, slightly calloused grip, steady eye contact.

'Any relation to Jacob?' said the older man.

'My brother.'

'Ah.' Hard to tell if Bruce Yi thought this was a good thing or not.

'You know Jake?' asked Luke.

'I know of him,' said Bruce. 'Jianne Xang is my brother-in-law's child. My niece.'

'Ah.' Awkward. 'Give Ji my regards,' said Luke quietly. He bore Ji no grudge. None of them did.

Okay, so maybe Jake bore her a *tiny* grudge for leaving

after less than a year of marriage and taking his heart with her. Luke was still pretty sure that Jake would be the first to say that his expectations of marriage and of Ji had been too high. Had Jake ever actually talked about his ill-fated marriage to anyone, that was. Which he hadn't.

'Curious, don't you think, that after all these years of separation neither Jacob nor Jianne has ever filed for a divorce?' said the older man with the searching eyes.

'I don't pretend to know my brother's mind,' said Luke. Bruce Yi would have to look elsewhere for his answers. 'And I certainly don't claim to know Ji's.'

'One can never truly know the mind of another,' said the older man. 'Still, one can speculate, can they not?'

'I'd rather not.'

Bruce Yi inclined his head and turned to Madeline. 'My wife has a new exhibition previewing on Friday evening. A small gathering only.'

'I'm sure Elena will put on a magnificent show,' said Madeline. 'She always does.'

'I'll add your name to the invitation list,' said Bruce. 'We'll hope to see you there.'

Madeline smiled but made no comment.

'You too, Mr Bennett.'

Madeline's silence seemed well worth emulating.

'Enjoy your meal,' said the older man, and with a nod resumed his course towards the door.

'Friend of yours?' said Luke once he'd taken his seat.

'No. One of Singapore's banking elite.' Madeline's eyes were unhappy, her features tight with tension. 'For the past six years, I've been consolidating Delacourte's assets. Now I'm ready to grow them. I have a development proposal with Yi Enterprises that needs strong financial backing and very specific partnerships. Bruce Yi can make it happen. I thought his overture was business related. I thought it was an invitation, in typical Chinese fashion, to start dealing. It wasn't. He's using me to get to you. He'll use you to get to Jacob.'

'That's quite an assumption,' said Luke. 'Given that until you introduced us he had no idea who I was.'

'He knew,' she said simply. 'Maybe he noticed your resemblance to Jake and hazarded a guess, maybe he knew some other way, but he stopped by this table because of you, not me.' She stared at him unhappily.

'And his invitation?'

'Should be viewed as an invitation to negotiate. I'm guessing that he wants Jianne's divorce finalised.'

'What's the project?' asked Luke. 'The one you want Bruce Yi to finance?'

'A Delacourte apartment-block build, our first major development in years, only this time we aim to incorporate onsite childcare, preschool, and early primary school facilities into the mix.'

'It doesn't sound risky to me.'

'We also want to fit a high-grade air-filtering system that'll give us a superior clean-air rating. They don't come cheap.'

'And you'll adjust your prices accordingly. Still not seeing a problem,' said Luke.

'The problem is me,' said Madeline bluntly. 'More specifically, Bruce Yi's perception of me. William was supposed to have had a stalwart first wife of good breeding who'd had the forethought to bear him children before being discarded. The bulk of the money would go to them. The problem being that William had no previous wife, children, or close family connections at all.'

'So you're the poster child for trophy wives,' said Luke with a shrug. 'So what?'

'So Bruce Yi still sees me as an upstart who got lucky. He doesn't see the businesswoman. He sees only what he wants to see.'

'Then change his mind.'

'How? By sacrificing you and Jacob to my ambition?'

'No, by attending this art preview, showing Bruce Yi your stripes as a visionary developer tycoon, and letting Jake and I take care of ourselves.'

Madeline shook her head ruefully. 'You don't understand. Bruce Yi doesn't *need* the Delacourte project. There are a dozen equally worthy proposals on his desk, all vying for his attention. He doesn't need anything from me except access to you. He's just made that very clear. And if I don't bring you…'

'Then bring me.'

'He's subtle.'

'You're annoying,' countered Luke. Nothing but the truth. 'Besides, I like a challenge. You said so yourself.'

'It'll be black tie.'

'I'll find one,' he said.

'I wouldn't put it past Bruce to arrange for Ji to be there.'

'And if you were trying to convince Jake to attend this function, that'd be the deal breaker. It's not a deal breaker for me.'

'I'd probably end up using you as a shield as well.'

'A shield against what?'

'Amorous intentions, mischief making, and the occasional dagger.'

'Has anyone ever told you that you make a lot of waves?'

'Frequently.' And if the shadows that fell across Madeline's eyes were any indication, it hadn't been delivered as praise. 'Forget it,' she said as the waiters descended with the food. 'You don't have to come. It's just a test.'

'In my experience, when people don't turn up for a test, they fail,' said Luke quietly. 'How about I put a mutually beneficial proposition to you?'

'I'm listening,' said Madeline, even if she wasn't looking at him. Instead she watched the comings and goings of the boats on the water. It provided a welcome alternative to watching and wanting the man who sat opposite her. He cut straight to the heart of things, this man. Straight to the heart of *her*.

Everyone had thought Delacourte would be bankrupt within a year of William's death, but Delacourte *hadn't* gone bankrupt, and that was her doing. If Madeline had her way she would see Delacourte growing again. The question was… At what cost? 'What did you have in mind?'

'You accompany me to the art exhibition and help me find out what Yi is thinking when it comes to Jake's affairs,' he said. 'If that puts you in a position to talk to him about your business initiatives, all the better. I don't mind mixing Bennett personal business with your profitable one.'

She glanced his way again and braced hard against the impact of such beauty of face and clarity of thought. 'Are you sure you're not Chinese?'

'No, but I do admire their ability to mix work and family business.'

'It's a skill that takes thousands of years of evolution,' said Madeline dryly. But for the first time since Bruce Yi had stopped by their table, Madeline actually considered attending the show. 'Are you sure?'

'Just say yes, Maddy, then pack Bruce Yi away in a box in that very clever brain of yours until Friday.'

'Because I don't think you quite know what you're in for.'

'I get that a lot,' he said drolly. 'Occupational hazard. I'm still not hearing a "yes".'

'All right, yes, and don't say I didn't warn you. Now what?'

'Now we go back to what we were doing before we were interrupted,' said Luke way too smoothly for comfort.

'Which was?'

The tiger smiled and sent a shaft of desire straight through her. 'Why, Maddy, I do believe you were admiring me.'

CHAPTER FIVE

SOME men had a way about them. Luke Bennett's way was nine tenths warrior, one tenth lazy suitor, and very nearly irresistible, decided Madeline as Luke paid for their meal and ushered her outside. He knew how to tease and he knew how to touch, his hand to the small of her back as he drew her closer to him to allow the passage of tourists walking the other way. Nothing proprietary about that touch, just a whole lot of warmth and protection that she missed when the pedestrians passed and his hand fell away.

They walked the waterfront and Madeline's need for more of his touch grew, and with it her tension. The rogue knew that she wanted his hands on her but the tiger seemed to sense a trap and the warrior chose to wait.

And wait.

He waited until they stood outside the private lift that would take them to her penthouse, and when it came and she asked him if he wanted to come up, he shrugged and stepped inside. When the lift arrived at its top-floor destination he made no move to get out. Instead he leaned back against the mirror and shoved his hands in his pockets, drawing the fabric of his trousers tight against a part of him no lady would be caught staring at.

Luke caught Madeline staring, and smiled.

'Would you like to come in for a coffee?' she said.

'It's not a good idea.'

She was well aware of that. But it hadn't stopped her asking.

'I can only play the gentleman up to a point, Maddy,' he said. 'If I came in, I'd want to stay until morning, and I'm really not sure I want to know what your house-keeper would serve up for breakfast.'

'If you're looking for excuses to stay away from me, you forgot to mention William's ghost and William's fortune,' she said.

Luke seared her with a glance. 'I believe I've already mentioned them. I'm still trying to decide if I can work my way around them. Don't push me, Maddy. Give me time.'

'Hey, you're the one who's only here for a week,' she murmured.

'Two.'

She smiled wryly. 'Sorry. Two.'

'Sometimes an explosive situation takes a lot longer to assess than you originally thought it would,' he said grimly. 'Sometimes you have to circle around it a while until you know what's going on.'

'And here I thought you were the reckless type.'

'Guess you were wrong,' he said. 'I'm *trying* to slow us down. You could try *helping* in that regard. Because God only knows where we'll end up if you don't.' His eyes glittered with a darkly sensual promise. 'You want to risk it?'

Suddenly, Luke's refusal to come in for coffee and whatever else she might have offered him seemed like a very good move. Vacating the elevator before giving in to the primitive edge of desire that swirled around them seemed like an even better one. 'No. You're right. No coffee and give my regards to the boys.' Madeline took a step back and put her finger to the control panel when the lift doors would have closed. 'Do you still want to attend the art exhibition together on Friday?'

He nodded.

'Okay, good. So I'll just…go.'

'Wait.' That deadly soft voice stopped her; flowed over her. 'You forgot something.'

'What?'

'Your goodnight kiss,' said Luke grimly and hauled her into his arms as the lift doors began to close. Surely, he thought as her lips opened beneath his, soft and warm and willing. Surely he wouldn't invite catastrophe with just one more little kiss.

And still her taste slammed through him, hot and wild and perfect. Still, his breath came hard and harsh and his body ached for just that little bit more when finally he released her.

'Go.'

Turning, Madeline pressed the button and waited for the lift doors to open once more, while every muscle screamed at her to turn around and lose herself in the white-hot desire to be found in Luke Bennett's arms. But he'd warned her not to unleash him, and it seemed a warning well worth heeding. For now.

She looked back as she stepped out—how could she

not? He stood leaning against the back wall again, with his hands in his pockets, his head thrown back, and his eyes were as hungry as hell. Madeline looked down over him as the lift doors began to close, looked down to where a lady really shouldn't look.

And smiled.

Friday came around quickly for Madeline. Bruce Yi had wasted no time in getting Elena to extend an invitation to the art exhibition; one invitation and two distinct names.

Bruce Yi's request for more information on the South Singapore apartment project arrived half an hour after Madeline had emailed Elena an acceptance to the gallery show on her and Luke's behalf.

Madeline had the information at her fingertips, all ready to go. She'd had it ready for weeks. Cursing, she stared at the folder and thought of the hope and ambitions it contained. Of the year of work that had already gone into visualising the project. Delacourte was ready for this project. *She* was ready, and it'd be so damned *easy* now that she had a card to play to simply play it, and get what she wanted out of the deal, and leave Jacob to fend for himself. Surely as the head of Delacourte Enterprises it was her job to be ruthless in the pursuit of profit? Luke had as good as *told* her to work Bruce Yi to her advantage and let Luke and Jacob take care of Bennett business. *Surely* Jacob could protect himself from Bruce Yi's machinations?

Couldn't he?

Damn, damn, and damn!

Madeline opened her desk drawer, shoved the file inside it, and slammed the drawer shut.

An empty desk now, and another stronger curse for good measure.

William had been the softest businessman in the world. He'd taught her many things during their time together, but ruthlessness hadn't been one of them. Madeline had been left to discover ruthlessness by herself in the wake of William's death. She'd had some tough decisions to make when it came to restructuring the company, what to keep and what to shed, but she'd made them, and worn them, and Delacourte had emerged the stronger for them.

Could she really abandon a ten-year friendship with one of the finest men she knew to the beast that was business?

A grim little smile twisted her lips. It would surprise no one if she did. She who'd married a soft touch for his money, buried him three years later, and never looked back. She who continued to play by rules no one else could fathom. The trophy wife who thought she had the wit to rebuild Delacourte. The woman who saw in a homeless street waif the spark of something pure and good and had known just the man who could take that spark and coax it into a strong and steady flame. The woman who loved the security that only extreme wealth could bring, but who nonetheless donated her annual wage to charity.

Delacourte made the money, paid Madeline and hundreds of others a wage, and Madeline gave her portion away. That was the way of it ever since William's death and the why of it was unfathomable even to her.

The workings of such a system, however, depended entirely on putting Delacourte Enterprises first. Everything else flowed on from that. That much she did know.

She'd already sacrificed love to the altar of financial security. Why not friendship too?

Round and round her thoughts went as the afternoon wore on. First one way and then the other.

Round and round again.

At four-thirty, Madeline put her office phone to her ear and called the dojo in search of Luke. When he wasn't around, she got his mobile number from Jake and called him direct.

'There's access to gallery parking at this show tonight. I thought I might take the car,' she said when Luke answered his phone. No need to mention that a goodly portion of her reasoning for wanting to take the car was a heartfelt desire to stay out of elevators that had Luke in them. 'So I'll swing by the dojo and collect you around seven? How does that sound?'

Silence. Then, 'Wrong,' muttered Luke dejectedly. 'So wrong in so many different ways.'

'Luke Bennett,' she scolded, thoroughly amused and not particularly surprised. 'Is this a money thing?'

'No, it's a car thing. The money thing is only a peripheral problem in this particular instance. The boy acquires a car. The boy picks the girl up in his car. The girl is impressed by the lad's ability to procure, drive, and run said car. The car is a metaphor for his ability to provide for her. That's how it works.'

'Quaint,' she said, smiling into the phone. 'What say I take your ability to provide all manner of things as read, and cut you a break seeing as you're a stranger in a foreign land and pick you up at seven?'

'What say I hire a car?' he said a touch desperately.

'Now why would you want to do that when I've a perfectly good vehicle sitting here practically unused?' she said sweetly. 'Would it help if I let you drive?'

'No, that would merely add insult to injury.'

'Whatever happened to equality of the sexes?'

'The Bennett boys opted out. What kind of car is it? No, let me guess. It's a pastel-coloured fuel-efficient compact.'

'It'd serve you right if it was,' said Madeline.

'It's not lime green with those smiley hubcaps that don't turn round, is it? Because if it is, we're walking.'

'It's a Mercedes convertible.' Madeline wasn't above a little teasing of her own. 'SL class, twelve purring little cylinders. Lots and lots of buttons to play with. You'll like it.' A strangled sound happened along the phone line. 'Luke Bennett, are you whimpering?'

'Yes, but only because the tailor just found my inside leg with a pin. It has nothing whatsoever to do with the thought of being picked up from my brother's house in *that* car by a woman whose wealth is vastly superior to my own. My ego is far more robust than that.'

'Of course it is. So I'll pick you up from the dojo at seven, then?'

'Whatever,' he said glumly.

'What colour's your suit?'

'Black.'

'Perfect.' Madeline smirked. 'You'll match the car.'

'Life is cruel,' said Luke and hung up.

'Just because a tiger purrs, doesn't mean you have to pet it.'

Yun's words of farewell rang in Madeline's ears as she

slid to a halt outside the dojo at seven that evening, ignoring the 'no parking' sign in favour of giving Po— who stood on sentry duty in the dojo doorway—a smile and a wave. Po smiled back and disappeared inside. Moments later Luke appeared and Madeline's heart thumped hard before settling into an irregular rhythm.

He'd been Navy once, she remembered, and those boys knew how to suit up when occasion demanded it. No discomfort from this man about wearing formal evening wear—just another uniform in a long line of uniforms that would help to get the job done.

Po skipped alongside Luke, a small boy with wide eyes as he stared first at Madeline and then at the convertible as Luke slipped in beside her.

'Jake said to tell you that if Luke's not home by midnight he'll think the worst,' said Po with a grin. 'He said you wouldn't want him to be thinking the worst because then he'd have to bust Luke's sorry arse.'

'Fair enough,' said Madeline.

'Easy for you to say.' Luke eyed Madeline darkly.

Po slipped back inside and Madeline eased out into the traffic with a discreet rumble. Luke studied her as she drove and she wondered what he saw. A nervous charlatan playing dress-ups or a confident woman who knew exactly who she was and what she wanted? Because when the Delacourte jewels went around her neck and the designer evening gown slid on, Madeline didn't feel confident and empowered at all. Mostly, she just felt vulnerable.

'Diamonds suit you,' he said finally, and Madeline shot him an uncertain smile.

'They belonged to William's grandmother.'

'They still suit you.'

'I like your suit,' she said.

'It has its uses.'

One of which was to drive her insane with wanting to peel him out of it.

'What do you know about Bruce Yi and his family?' asked Luke next.

Solid ground. Finally. 'Elena is Bruce's first wife, which is something of a rarity for a man of his wealth and age. Elena's family is practically Shanghai royalty. Bruce Yi's lineage is equally impressive but Singapore based. Word has it that the marriage was an arranged one. Somewhere along the way it became a happy one.'

'Any children?'

'Two sons, our age. They work for their father. They work hard for him. No free rides there.'

'Are the sons in relationships?'

'Never for long. They play as hard as they work.' Madeline thought back to the family relationships Bruce Yi had spoken of the other night. Of Ji being Elena's brother's child. 'So Ji's a Shanghai Xang?'

Luke nodded.

'That's serious wealth.' Wealth enough to more than match the Delacourte family fortune. 'How did Jake cope with that?'

'You mean when he finally found out?' said Luke dryly. 'Not well.'

'I can imagine,' she murmured. 'Was that the reason their marriage failed?'

Luke shrugged. 'One of them, maybe. But there were

other difficulties. Other responsibilities that Jake had to shoulder that got in the way of a marriage.'

Whatever they were, Luke didn't offer them up. Instead he changed the subject. 'You said you and your brother were wards of the state. When did that happen?'

'My mother died when I was seven. My brother was four. My father drank himself to death a year or so later.' She offered the information up as fact, no sympathy required, and no real expectation of Luke's understanding.

There was no way to describe the desperation that came of growing up in the care of the state. No money, no permanent home, no control. She hadn't even been able to keep Remy with her. Only what would fit into a carry case and the dreams she'd carried in her head. *One day when I'm old enough... One day when I'm rich... One day when I'm loved...*

Madeline lifted a hand from the steering wheel and lightly touched her necklace. That someone, anyone, could love her had come as such a shock. William's innate kindness had simply sealed the deal.

'It's still there,' said Luke gently. 'The necklace.'

Silently, Madeline returned her hand to the wheel.

'My mother died when I was thirteen,' said Luke next in a rusty voice that bespoke a topic usually avoided. 'My father's still alive, but he wasn't much of a father for a while. There were five of us kids, and we were luckier than you. We got to stay together. We had a house. We had a father in residence, at least on paper. Occasionally, he even remembered to pay the bills. And the four of us younger ones...we had Jake.'

'I'm glad,' she murmured, and drove in silence until they reached the skyscraper that housed the first-floor gallery. She drove down into the underground car park, took one look at the bank of lifts and parked by the stairs. The stairs would bring them out onto the street level. Glass doors would take them into the building, and an escalator would take them directly to the gallery door. Luke would doubtless enjoy a little Orchid Road sightseeing far more than he'd enjoy looking at the inside of yet another lift.

She couldn't be alone in a lift with Luke Bennett right now. Not without reaching for him. Not without wanting him far more than she should.

Luke strode through the luxury marble-and-glass foyer without really admiring it. He liked having enough money that he would never go homeless or hungry. He didn't see a whole lot of appeal in courting the kind of wealth that Madeline and the Yi family administered on a daily basis, no matter how sweet their rides.

He was here for his brother, and maybe—almost certainly—he was here because he couldn't stay away from Madeline Delacourte, she of the unwieldy bank balance and gut-wrenching vulnerability. He'd seen the broken child in her eyes when she'd offered up her brief childhood history. He'd seen it in the uncertainty with which she wore those shiny stones. He got it now, he finally got an inkling of why wealth and power ruled her.

The homeless child demanded it.

That same child who hadn't been able to walk past Po without doing something to help him.

The child tore at his heart. The woman the child had become had the capacity to steal it from him whole.

An art show.

Lord save him, this wasn't his world.

'Ready?' she said lightly.

To fall in love with her? 'Not in the slightest,' he said as they stepped off the escalator and approached the door, where a weather-beaten little peacock of a man stood waiting beside a podium that might normally be used to display a menu but tonight held only a list of names.

'Madeline Delacourte,' the man said, with what looked to be genuine delight. 'It's my pleasure to see you out and about again. It's been too long.'

'Arthur,' said Madeline in reply, and bestowed on him a polished smile. 'You rogue. What are you doing here?'

'My job,' said Arthur. 'You're looking at Gallery One's latest curator.' The little rogue peacock put his palm to his chest. 'Arthur,' he said grandly, 'has fallen on his feet.'

'Congratulations,' said Madeline, and turned towards Luke, as if conscious of having left him out of the conversation. 'William was very fond of acquiring antique Chinese porcelain pieces. Arthur was very fond of finding them for him. The last piece Arthur found for him was a magnificent funeral vase which cost a small fortune, even by William's standards.'

'Ah, but it was a masterpiece,' said Arthur. 'Was it not?'

'Indeed it was, and I have to say it came in very handy.'

Arthur blanched. 'You didn't.'

'Oh, but I did,' said Madeline with an amused smile, and sashayed through the sliding glass doors.

Sparing a searching glance for the shell-shocked doorman, Luke followed her into the gallery and played the part of companion and helped Madeline remove her light-weight wrap.

'I take it William's currently resting in the funeral vase,' he murmured.

'He was very fond of it,' said Madeline. 'It seemed the least I could do.'

'You didn't…?' Luke knew a little something of Chinese funeral vases—most of it gleaned from his sister. He shook his head. 'Never mind.'

'Never mind what?'

'Nothing. Except…'

Madeline waited expectantly for him to finish.

'How did William die?'

'It was very strange,' she said. 'He stepped out onto the road unexpectedly and got run over by a truck.'

Luke stepped back and handed Madeline her wrap. They made their way towards the first painting, a white circle on a black background, with a smaller black blob dead centre of the white circle, and bright red squiggles radiating from its centre. It looked like a drunkard's eyeball and Luke would definitely not want to wake up to it every morning.

The price tag made him grin.

He tilted his head and studied the painting some more. No, not a drunkard's eyeball. A *dead* man's eyeball. 'A truck, you say?'

'Mmm.' Madeline moved on to the next picture. More blobs, different colours, with a fork sticking out of the centre. 'I'm really not seeing the symbolism,' she murmured.

'That's okay.' Luke was seeing more than enough symbolism for both of them. 'So…William buys a funeral vase—'

'Actually, I bought the funeral vase, even though William chose it. It was a birthday gift.'

Luke shuddered. 'So *you* buy William a funeral vase…and then he gets run over by a truck and dies.'

Madeline turned to stare at him, amused incredulity writ plain on her face. 'Luke Bennett, are you superstitious?'

'No,' he muttered darkly as a tiny, dark-haired matron dressed in sleek dove grey approached them. 'Not precisely.'

'Elena,' said Madeline with a smile. 'Always a pleasure.'

'When Bruce told me he'd seen you out and about I rejoiced for you,' said Elena, with what sounded like sincerity. 'Six years is too long a time for a young widow to cloister herself away from society.' The woman turned to Luke, her eyes sharp and assessing. 'And you must be Luke.'

'Yes, ma'am.'

'Jianne said yours was the most beautiful family of warriors she'd ever seen. I've never met Jacob, but if he's anything like you I think she must have spoken true.' Elena's gaze cut back to Madeline. 'Is it true?'

'I've only ever met Jacob and Luke,' said Madeline. 'So far it's true.'

Elena sighed. Bruce Yi materialised beside his wife and greeted Madeline and Luke with warm cordiality. 'What do you make of the paintings?' he said.

'We've only just begun to look at them,' said Madeline smoothly.

'Who knew an art show could be so enlightening?' added Luke.

'Bruce, why don't you introduce Madeline to those project managers you wanted her to meet?' said Elena. 'Luke can stay here with me for a time.'

Divide and conquer. Luke knew the ploy well. He wasn't the middle child of five for nothing. Madeline shot him a questioning glance. Luke gave a tiny nod of assent. Go, he told her silently. Go do business.

'I tried to persuade Jianne to attend the reception this evening,' said Elena as they strolled slowly towards the next painting. 'She's over from Shanghai and visiting with us at the moment. Alas, she had a prior engagement.'

Luke said nothing, just watched Madeline move off, with an innate elegance and dignity about her that he doubted she even knew she had.

'She does send you her fondest regards,' said the little raven.

'She has mine,' said Luke.

'It could be that Jianne will choose to reside in Singapore permanently, soon.'

Now there was a comment to capture his attention. He wrenched his gaze away from Madeline and focused on what Elena Yi had to say. 'Ji has business here?' More to the point, would Singapore be big enough for both Jake and Ji?

'Not exactly,' said Elena as they moved on to view the next painting. 'I rather suspect she's moving away from something unpleasant, as opposed to actively moving towards something good.'

Luke smiled wryly. 'She does that.'

Auntie's eyes flashed. Luke didn't give a damn.

'My brother,' said the little raven, 'Jianne's father, wishes to see his daughter remarried.'

'To who?' said Luke.

'The only son of a business associate.'

'So it's a business merger?'

Elena nodded. 'A very profitable one for both families.'

'Are you asking Jake for a divorce on Jianne's behalf?'

'No,' said Elena quietly as they stared at yet another painting. Two sets of circles within circles this time. Demon's eyes. 'I want him to save her from that monster.'

'Mr Yi, before you introduce me to these people I need you to know something,' said Madeline, knowing her next move for business suicide but knowing too that she'd made up her mind and would not relax until she'd spoken.

Bruce Yi looked at her but kept right on walking.

'I have no influence over Luke Bennett or his brother so whatever you want from them, I can't help you get it. Even if I could influence them to your advantage, I wouldn't.'

'Why not?'

Madeline smiled ruefully. 'Because Jacob Bennett's a friend. He's also one of the finest men I know, and I'm sorry but I won't let you use me to get to him.'

'Not even to grow Delacourte?'

'I'll find another way to grow Delacourte. I like big business, Mr Yi. I'm usually quite good at it.' Tonight, of course, being the exception.

This time Bruce Yi stopped. Madeline stopped too, and squared up to him, eye to eye. 'I can't help you,' she said quietly.

'Then why are you here?'

'Because Luke wants to find out what you want. What Ji wants. From Jacob.'

'Rest assured, Madeline. He will.'

Madeline glanced back at Luke and Elena, who looked deep in conversation, but even as Madeline looked away Luke glanced at her, those golden eyes dark and guarded.

'My wife has more finesse in these matters than I do,' said Bruce Yi. 'Women generally have more patience with such things, although you certainly don't seem to. You should have waited, Madeline. You should have waited to see whether Jacob Bennett's needs coincided with those of the house of Yi.'

Yes, well. Too late now.

'Honour is a rare and admirable quality in this world of changing values,' continued Bruce Yi, he of the thin-lipped smile and the sharp, sharp eyes. 'But I've always found it best when served with patience. Come.' Bruce waylaid a passing waiter and moments later Madeline found herself with a champagne in hand. 'I would have you meet my business partners. It will save time should we ever decide to do business together.'

Reprimanded and outmanoeuvred in one smooth stroke, Madeline sipped at her champagne. She learned fast when it came to the machinations of big business, but there was no denying that the head of the house of Yi had at least a thirty-year head start.

Time to lift her game.

Squaring her shoulders and summoning a smile, Madeline turned her mind to business.

CHAPTER SIX

'HAD enough?' asked Luke as he materialised by Madeline's side some half an hour later.

'More than enough.' The paintings weren't to her taste, Bruce Yi's partners had grilled her to within an inch of incineration about her future business plans, the Delacourte diamonds hung heavy around her neck, and, above all, she was *hungry*.

They found their hosts and said their goodbyes. Elena looked pale and anxious. Luke looked grim. Madeline badly wanted to be outside where there was warmth and air, or back at the dojo where there was honesty and care. Not this. She didn't like the strain inherent in this inter-action, even if everyone *was* on their best behaviour.

Madeline unclasped her necklace and slipped off her earrings as they descended the escalator. 'Got an inside pocket in that jacket of yours?' she asked Luke.

Luke unbuttoned his jacket silently as she turned towards him. He did have one, and it even had a button to keep it closed. Fiddly thing.

'You get the button, I'll hold the rocks,' he murmured, so she dumped them in his palm and set to work easing that stubborn little button through its buttonhole. The jacket felt warm to the touch, Luke's formal white shirt—as the backs of her fingers brushed over it—felt even warmer. Plenty of heat inside this jacket. Plenty of hard and corded muscle beneath that fine white shirt.

They stepped off the escalator and stepped to one side of it while Luke slipped the jewellery in the pocket and Madeline buttoned it back up, before pressing his jacket closed and buttoning *that* up.

There. Those jewels were as safe as they were going to get, and for now, Madeline was free of their weight.

'Care to tell me *why* the jewellery had to come off now?' he murmured, watching her through guarded golden eyes.

'There's a tapas bar around the corner,' she said. Misdirection being by far the better option than confessing how truly undeserving the Delacourte diamonds made her feel. 'It's not exactly classy but the food is good and the atmosphere's relaxed and I need both of those elements right now. It's not the place for diamonds.' She tried a smile.

Luke didn't return it.

'Or we could head straight home if you'd rather get back and talk to Jacob. He's probably waiting to hear from you. I'm sorry. I didn't think—'

'It's okay,' he muttered. 'I haven't said anything to Jake about meeting Bruce Yi. Yet. Jake's big on inner harmony and peace. I figured I'd wait until I had something concrete to offer by way of information before I shattered the calm.'

'Protective,' she murmured.

'When it comes to my family's well-being, yes. You have a problem with that?'

'No.'

The tapas bar was darkly sexy and deliberately intimate. Neckwear seemed optional, and, given that Maddy had already ditched hers, Luke loosened his tie and undid the buttons of his shirt collar so that a man might breathe in comfort. Madeline smiled wry approval at him as they found a couple of seats at the bar. Madeline took a perch. Luke elected to stand.

'You wear black tie extremely well, don't get me wrong,' she said. 'But you wear informality better.'

'Says the woman who wears diamonds as if she were born to them and then ditches them the minute she can. Personally, I prefer you without,' he countered. 'Did you get what you wanted from Bruce Yi?'

'I've no idea.' The barman headed their way and they ordered drinks and tapas. The drinks came fast and the food order went in. 'Did Elena say what Ji wanted of Jacob?' Madeline asked him.

'No, but she did say what *she* wanted of Jake. She seems to want him back in Ji's life. Says it's for Ji's protection.' Luke studied her intently. 'How many months after you bought the vase did William die?'

'A year or so,' said Madeline, blinking at the rapid change of topic. 'What *is* it with you and William's funeral vase? I assure you, the funeral and the cremation—everything happened as it should. It's not as if I torched him.'

'Never mind,' said Luke with a shake of his head as he

took to his beer and drank deeply. 'It's nothing. I'm over it.' Mostly. Could Madeline really have it in her to arrange her husband's demise? He thought not. Definitely not. Probably just a coincidence, her purchase of a funeral vase…

Curators like Arthur sold antique funeral vases to wealthy collectors all the time.

And delivered them empty.

Tapas, champagne, and Luke Bennett's company made for an easy combination, and Madeline let herself relax into the evening and bask in the warmth of those gleaming tiger eyes. He'd surprised Madeline tonight with his ability to move comfortably through Bruce Yi's world of high finance and high-priced art but there was no mistaking that he was more at home here. So was she, truth being told. She'd never courted high society, for all that she'd experienced her fair share of it at William's side. She'd never returned to it after his death.

An orphan's sensitivity for knowing she would find little welcome there.

A woman's dislike of moving through such a world unprotected.

She hadn't been unprotected tonight. Bruce Yi, in the making of important introductions and staying on to guide the conversation, had extended his protection and made sure others noticed it.

And Luke, with his watchful warrior presence, had offered his.

It was enough to send a sensible woman's thoughts tripping down roads they really shouldn't go. A short-term light-hearted relationship was the only way to travel when it came to dealing with this man. To consider even that much was risky.

'Tell me,' she said lightly. 'If you had a family of your own one day—a wife and children—would you still disarm weapons for a living?'

'It's what I do,' he said. 'What else would I do?'

'I don't know. Ship salvage work? Return to your deep-diving roots? Something safer.'

'Neither of the occupations you just suggested are particularly safe, Maddy.'

'Maybe not, but I really can't see you in an office. I was extrapolating backwards just a step or two.'

'Thanks,' he said dryly. 'The salvage work I could do. It just wouldn't have quite the bite of what I do now.'

'What do your siblings think about your choice of career and the dangers involved?'

'You mean the brother who pilots air-sea rescue Seahawks or the one who runs black ops for Interpol? Or are you asking me what Jake thinks?'

Madeline wasn't sure she wanted to know what any of them thought. 'What does your *sister* think?'

'She thinks we're all guts and glory. She retaliated by marrying a computer whiz with brains instead.' Luke's grin came wide and wicked. 'He does a little creative programming for Interpol on the side these days.'

'Bet that went down a bomb.'

'You have no idea,' said Luke with a shudder. 'Carnage.'

'Are your other brothers married?'

Luke nodded. 'And before you ask, Tris removed himself voluntarily from fieldwork and took a desk job once he got married but Pete still flies air-sea rescue missions. Pete had a habit of not phoning Serena the minute he set foot back on land. Serena broke that particular habit by getting her own helicopter licence so she could have better access to remote photographic locations. She accidentally lost radio contact one day when she went up alone. She was in a dead zone and she knew it, but she stuck around for a twilight shot and didn't get home until well after dark.'

'Simple yet effective,' said Madeline. 'I like it.'

'Absolutely ruthless,' said Luke. 'The man was a wreck.'

'And what do *you* do when the woman you're with has trouble accepting your work?' she asked.

'Move on.' His eyes grew shuttered. 'Nothing else I can do.'

Except give up the work. A concept he clearly had trouble with. 'Don't you ever get sick of living so close to the edge of death?' she asked quietly. 'Don't you ever look at a situation sometimes and wish you could just walk away and leave it to someone else?'

'No,' he said, but the shadows in his eyes told a deeper, darker story. 'Not if I'm the best person for the job. I'm not in the phone book, Maddy. My name is on half a dozen lists worldwide. When someone contacts me it means that they need my particular skill set and they need it fast. There's no defence against that. I can't just say, "Sorry, I don't feel like working today." I can't.'

A warrior's honour, soul deep and absolute. Duty-bound, forsaking all else.

Hard not to admire such a man.

Madness to love him.

He looked at her in silent enquiry. 'Another drink?'

'No, I'm driving.'

'Ready to head home?'

'I think I am,' she said solemnly. 'I can drop you on the way.'

But he shook his head. 'That's not how it works, Maddy. Not with me. I'll see you home. I'll see you to your door. And then I'll find my own way back to Jake's.'

Chivalry. Cousin to honour. She should have guessed he'd have his share of that too.

The trip home was largely silent after that, as if Luke sensed her withdrawal or her conflict, or both. They made it to the apartment car park and headed for the lift.

Last time in this lift, Luke had been the one to hold back.

This time she hoped to God she would be the one to walk away. They entered the lift and she stared at the ground. If she didn't look at him, didn't touch him, and didn't talk to him, she'd probably be just fine.

The lift rose quickly and then slid to a halt. The doors slid open.

Time to end this madness.

Some sort of farewell comment seemed in order. 'Goodbye, Luke. I've enjoyed getting to know you.' She hoped she'd made it sound final enough.

'You forgot something,' he said.

'No.' She risked a glance and cursed her foolishness as warmth suffused her body. 'No, I haven't.'

'Your diamonds,' he said as he unbuttoned his jacket. 'Unless you'd like me to send Po round with them tomorrow? Probably not a good idea, though.'

Oh. Right. The diamonds. The ones in his inside coat pocket. Madeline hesitated. Luke shook his head, his eyes dark and knowing. He shrugged out of his jacket and handed it to her whole. 'I know you've decided not to see me again, Maddy. I can see it in your eyes. It's okay. I'm used to it.'

'All that honour,' she said raggedly as she battled with the recalcitrant button and buttonhole. 'Where did you *get* it?'

He shrugged and his lips tilted towards a wry smile. 'Beats me.'

'We wouldn't be any good together, you and me.' The button was stuck. The pocket stayed closed. Where was Po when you needed him? 'We're too different.'

'Who are you trying to convince, Maddy? Me? Or yourself?'

She gave up on the button. 'I mean, look at you.' She made the mistake of doing just that and the need inside her soared. 'You need a woman whose honour can equal your own. A woman with strength enough to let you go when you have to go and do what you need to do. I can't even manage honour, let alone the strength I'd need to love you.'

'Tell me something, Maddy,' he said in that quiet, deadly voice. 'Tonight, when you and Bruce Yi stopped to talk, just before you reached his business partners. What did you say to him?'

'Not a lot.'

'You told him you couldn't guarantee my or Jake's co-operation, didn't you? And you elected out of the deal he was setting up.'

'It didn't feel right.'

'You want to know why?'

Madeline shrugged. 'An aversion to debt?'

A tiny shake of his head while his golden gaze kept her frozen to the spot. 'Honour.'

'It could have gone either way,' she said raggedly. 'If it was honour you thought you saw, then I almost abandoned it.'

'But you didn't. I don't see weakness when I look at you,' he said softly. 'I see generosity and grace, and I see strength and survival.' He came towards her then. He came to stand within an inch of her. 'And I want it.'

The jacked slipped through suddenly nerveless fingers to land on the floor beside her.

'Trouble is, you have to want me too,' he said. 'And seeing as you don't—'

She didn't let him finish. Instead she found his mouth with her own, frantic need ruling her as she took what she wanted and drank deeply of this man. All that devastating integrity wrapped within a reckless smile...she wanted it all and to hell with tomorrow.

Luke knew only one response to attack, be it sensual or otherwise. Counter-attack, using whatever weapons he had at hand. He didn't seek to quell Madeline's need for his kisses, he grew it until her breath came in gasps between open-mouthed kisses and her hands were buried in his hair. His hands roved where they would. One hand cradling her head and the other at her back, gathering her close, snaking down her spine.

The sweet curve of her buttocks deserved two hands, but by then she'd entwined her arms around his neck and his lips were at her throat, passion riding them both hard as he lifted her up and she wound her legs around his waist.

Her back met the wall, the handrail providing a tiny ledge on which to balance her while her fingers worked frantically to undo the buttons of his shirt and he hiked her dress up to her waist. Luke's shirt came off, he damn near ripped it off in his effort to accommodate her.

'This isn't going to work,' she whispered, and then her hands were at his chest, and her lips were at his throat and he surrendered completely to his desperate need for more. 'Not in the long run.'

'I'm hearing you. I'm *agreeing* with you.' He edged her panties aside and showed her exactly where he wanted in. 'Damned if I know what to do with you.'

There, right there, thought Madeline with a whimper, and his touch was slow and sure and devastatingly effective. She moved on him then, onto his hand, with the fleshy base of his thumb to her nub and his finger easing inside her.

The woman she glimpsed in the side mirror was an abandoned stranger, her eyes glazed, her lips swollen, and her hair in disarray as she rocked slowly back and forth against the hand of a man she'd met less than a week ago.

Dark edged and warrior savage, Luke took her hand and dragged it down and over his trousers. So hard and huge as she shaped her hand around him and followed his long length down to the source and back to where belt met buckle and head nestled beneath. She managed to get the belt undone, and then the button and zip, which gave her all the access she needed as he claimed her mouth again.

There was no finesse in him as he lifted her high and brought her down onto him and held her tight. Madeline gasped and buried her face in his shoulder as she adjusted to his possession.

Tight. She was so warm and tight. One arm at her back and one in her hair as need pushed Luke further and harder into her, too far in thrall to be a gentleman. Too far gone to care that they were in an elevator. And then she bit down hard on the cord of his neck, not gentle but ravenous, and the wildness he carried deep down inside him rose up and finally broke free.

Raw power and desperation, as she matched him need for need.

White heat and exaltation as she cried out her release.

Red haze and incantation as he rode her hard and exploded deep inside her.

That they'd remained upright when they'd lost their minds seemed something of a miracle to Luke. That Madeline still clung to him seemed even more of a miracle. He put his forehead to hers, breathing hard as he closed his eyes and tried to remember how they'd come to this.

'Maddy,' he murmured, when he had the words for speech. 'Maddy, I'm sorr—'

'Don't,' she said, and covered his mouth with trembling fingers. Her lips replaced her fingers, softer still and even more vulnerable. 'Don't be.'

So he kissed her again, as gently as he could, and even then the bite of hunger raised its head and threatened to overpower him.

He pulled out of the kiss, and put his lips to her temple instead.

He looked in the mirror at what he'd done and closed his eyes, not ready to face the truth of it.

'I wish…' What did he wish? That the last five minutes hadn't happened? No, he didn't wish that. 'I should have taken better care of you.' He shouldn't have lost control.

'I've no complaints.' He tasted the truth in her words. He opened his eyes to find her watching him solemnly.

'None,' she said with a shrug. 'I wanted this. Wanted you, in spite of all those very good reasons to stay away from you. I may not know where all this is heading, but I'm big girl enough to take plenty of responsibility for how we got here.'

Even as Madeline finished her speech, body parts rippled and twitched. Madeline's lashes came down to cover her eyes and she caught at her swollen lower lip with her teeth.

'Aftershock?' he murmured, in that dark knowing voice.

'Mmm.'

'More?'

'Please.'

Madeline whimpered as her legs closed vicelike around him and she ground down hard. A not so gentle thrust, the brush of his thumb, and she tilted her head back, and came for him again.

Hot colour stained her cheeks when finally she deigned to open her eyes.

'Would you like me to kiss it better?' he murmured silkily. 'Because, trust me, all you have to do is ask.'

Inner muscles jumped for him again and Luke hardened, feeling invincible. Half a dozen slow and rocking strokes, an open-mouthed kiss that imprinted itself somewhere in the vicinity of his heart, and he came deep inside her again.

Madeline emerged from Luke's latest possession bone-less, and damn near mindless. By some miracle they were still standing, but Luke's chest heaved with the effort of drawing breath and he stood shoulder slumped to the mirrored wall in what she suspected was a valiant attempt not to crush her.

His eyes were closed; his grin was wide. 'You know how you said you got us into this?' he murmured, his voice a throaty purring rumble. 'Any ideas on how to get us *out*?'

'Not one.' A functioning brain was not one of her current assets. 'I got nothing.' Nothing that didn't involve extreme mortification on her part. 'You *do* realise that I'm never going to be able to step into this elevator again without thinking of you?'

Luke's grin widened. Clearly not his problem. He opened sleepy eyes, gleaming gold against sable lashes. 'Take the stairs.'

'That would require me finding my feet,' she said. 'I'm not entirely sure that's possible.'

'It has to be,' he murmured. 'Because if we stay here like this much longer, chances are I'm going to drop you.'

He eased out of her and slid her down his body until her feet touched the ground. His hands came up to frame her face. Big hands. Gentle hands, as he urged her closer and into the sweetest of kisses.

'I'll make a deal with you,' he murmured. 'If you don't overthink what just happened, neither will I.'

'It's a good deal, don't get me wrong,' she said as she straightened her dress down over her stomach and thighs and clamped her knees together. 'I'll think about it.'

He fastened his trousers, buttoned his shirt, and bent down to pick up his jacket. He kissed her again, no hands just lips, and she responded again. She had the disturbing suspicion that she would always respond to this man's kisses.

He deftly unbuttoned his inside jacket pocket and retrieved the Delacourte diamonds, before letting the jacket drop to the floor once more. He separated necklace and earrings and dumped the earrings in her hand.

'Turn around,' he said, and draped the diamonds around her neck. Madeline slipped the earrings back on and stared at the picture she and Luke made in the mirror. Tousled and wanton, the pair of them. Satiated and surrounded by the warm scent of sex.

'Is your housekeeper in residence this evening?' he said.

'Uh-huh.'

Luke winced. 'Can you walk?' he asked next as he pressed the button that would open the lift doors.

'I can shuffle.' Thighs and knees firmly locked together might be best, otherwise the scent of sex was going to get a whole lot stronger.

He looked at her with the faintest of grins before scooping her up with one arm behind her knees and the other around her waist as he strode from the lift. He deposited her on her feet at the door, tucked a wisp of her hair behind her ear, and draped her wrap around her neck, his eyes warm as he nodded his approval. 'Perfect,' he said. 'I'm pretty sure she won't notice a thing.'

Madeline was pretty sure he was joking. 'You're not coming in?'

'Well, I *would*,' he said. 'But no.'

Madeline narrowed her eyes. 'Luke Bennett, are you scared of my housekeeper?'

'Shouldn't I be?' he said.

'Well, yes. But that's beside the point. I put out for you in a *lift*.'

'The recollection of which is burned into my brain,' he said in all sincerity.

'But you won't even come into my house?'

The house paid for by her late husband. The husband whose ashes probably sat in a vase on a mantelpiece somewhere. The husband Luke railed against, even though everything he'd heard about the man and Madeline's relationship with him had been good. 'It's complicated.'

'It's not that complicated,' said Madeline darkly. 'Is this about William?'

'Partly. I can't compete with him money-wise, Maddy. You know that.'

'I'm not asking you to.'

'Then try this for a reason.' Luke gave it to her straight. 'I'm scared. I'm dead scared of what I feel for you and what I'll do for you. Coffee I can do. The rest of the night I can do. The rest of the week I can do, here with you. But one day my phone's going to ring and I'll have to go and if you ask me to stay you're going to break me in two. So you be sure, Maddy. You be damn sure before you invite me any further into your life that you know what you're getting us into.'

He headed for the lift. She didn't call him back. Straight backed and fiery eyed, she glared at him.

'I wish to hell I'd never laid eyes on you,' she muttered.

'Try wishing to heaven instead,' he said grimly. 'I hear they're a lot better at giving people what they want.'

CHAPTER SEVEN

'Well, well, well,' said Jake as Luke strode into the tiny dojo kitchen at five past twelve. 'Aren't you looking all loose limbed and relaxed.'

Luke checked his clothing. Nothing wrong there. Not a lot he could do about his current looseness of limb either, except wait for it to wear off. As for baring his soul to Jake, no, no, and no. He didn't even want to *think* about what he and Madeline had started tonight, let alone talk about it. He really didn't. 'Bite me.'

Jake's gaze slid to his neck. 'Someone has.'

Luke stared him down in silence.

Jake's lips twitched, but he made no further comment.

Luke headed for the fridge and pulled out a couple of beers.

'Pass,' said Jake as Luke set one of them down in front of him.

Luke briefly considered putting Jake's beer back in the fridge, but sooner or later this conversation was going to swing round to Ji. Luke let the unwanted beer stand where it was.

'Did you know that Maddy's husband stepped onto the

road unexpectedly, got run over by a truck, and died?' Luke asked his brother.

'Happens I did,' said Jake.

'And that Maddy had bought him an empty funeral vase a year earlier?'

Jake blinked. Then he began to grin. 'You can't think that had anything to do with his death?'

Luke set the beer to his lips and slaked his thirst before answering. 'Why not? Maybe purchasing the vase initiated a contract that got fulfilled a year later. It's not as if those kinds of processes aren't in place—look what happened with Hallie and Nick.'

Jake was laughing outright now at the mention of their sister and her similar experience with such a funeral vase. 'You think Maddy bought the vase, offed her husband and yet you *still* had sex with her? How does that work, exactly?'

Luke opened his mouth. He closed it again without speaking because there was sure as hell nothing to say. The memory of being inside Maddy in the lift closed in on him, turning him twitchy, and lazily, impossibly alert. He didn't smile. But he wanted to.

'Man, you are so screwed,' said Jake.

'Yeah, well. I'm not the only one,' said Luke, retaliation being a perfectly reasonable form of defence, not to mention the kind he vastly preferred. 'We started the evening at an art show hosted by Bruce and Elena Yi. You know them?'

'No. Should I?'

'Probably. They're Jianne's aunt and uncle. And they sure as hell know of you.'

Jake shrugged. 'Lucky them.'

'I spoke to Elena Yi for a while,' offered Luke carefully. 'It seemed only polite considering she'd gone to some lengths to arrange the meeting. She seems to think that Ji's in trouble.'

Not by a flicker did Jake's emotions show on his face. But he reached for the beer Luke had left on the table, and cracked it and drank deeply before replying. 'What kind of trouble?'

'Ji's father wants her to marry some business associate of his. Ji's aunt thinks the man's a monster. She'd like to cut this monster out of Ji's life completely, hence the need for a hero. She'd prefer you to appear on a white charger, if at all possible. Judging by the madness of those paintings tonight, I figure any colour of horse will do.'

Jake sat back in his chair and ran a hand through his hair. He put his beer to his lips and Luke let his brother be. Jake had always been the calm one, the unflappable leader of their family unit, but that didn't make him an ice man. All it did was make him more dangerous than the rest of them put together on those rare times that his emotional levee finally did break.

'What does Ji want?' said Jake finally.

'I don't know.' Luke reached into his back pocket, pulled out a business card and slid it across the table. 'But she's staying with her aunt and uncle in Singapore at the moment, and that's their private number. You could always call her and find out.'

Jake stared at the glossy red card with its ivory-coloured embossed Chinese characters. He didn't pick it up. 'She could just be batty,' he said. 'The aunt. I mean a monstrous suitor and a dynasty princess in need of saving? It's a scene ripped straight from a fairy tale.'

'Well, the uncle's crazy, then, too,' said Luke. 'Because he's backing his wife all the way.'

Madeline slept fitfully, rose early, and found herself at work by seven. Her personal office staff didn't work weekends, and truth being told Madeline had no real need to be there other than to reassure herself that the security she craved still existed and that she had full control of it.

Better this than lazing in bed and recalling what it was like to surrender herself into the arms of a passionate warrior. A crusader who stared death in the face every time he took a job. A lover who surrendered to pleasure with an intensity that reeked of no tomorrows.

Better to bury herself in work than contemplate a body replete.

Far wiser to forget all about Luke Bennett's hungry lovemaking than to acknowledge—with the dismay of a junkie who already knew after only one hit—that life had just changed irrevocably.

When her office phone rang at five minutes past nine, Madeline stared at it for at least half a dozen rings before finally picking up and speaking her name.

The pregnant silence on the other end of the phone wasn't exactly encouraging. 'Hello?'

'Mrs Delacourte?' said a soft female voice. 'My name's Jianne Xang.'

Oh.

'You went to my aunt and uncle's gallery presentation last night. With Luke Bennett.'

'Yes,' said Madeline. 'Yes, I know.' God help her.

'I was hoping I could get a contact number for him from you.'

Oh. 'I have a number for him on my mobile if you'd care to wait while I retrieve it.' Madeline didn't know what to say of what she knew of Ji's relationship with the Bennetts. Which admittedly wasn't much. 'Another way to contact him would be to call his brother's dojo. That's where he's staying. At Jake's. You could try calling him there?'

Awkward silence.

'Hang on, I'll grab my mobile.'

'Shi shi ni,' said Jianne. A polite thank you.

Madeline gave the woman Luke's number.

Jianne thanked her again, in English this time, and hung up.

Madeline took one look at the Delacourte apartment project filing cabinet full of plans that might never see the light of day and promptly put her elbows to the desk and her hands to her face. Surely her role in the Jake and Jianne Xang saga had come to an end, hadn't it? Contact had been established between representatives of the two families. Messages had been sent. Hundred-million-dollar deals had been blown. What more could they possibly want from her?

Apart from a phone number.

The phone rang again. Madeline groaned. If Jianne Xang wanted the dojo number she could have that too. Maybe Jake would thank her one day. Maybe Ji and Jake would get back together, Bruce Yi would deign to do business with her, Delacourte would start to grow again, and Luke would stop disarming weaponry for a living.

And maybe she was dreaming.

'Your housekeeper gave me your work number. I think I'm growing on her.' Luke's voice on the other end of the phone line, sparking a head full of memories of last night in his company. Before the elevator, and in it. After the elevator, and the way they'd parted. Not amicably.

'Hey,' she said warily. It was better than saying nothing at all.

'Ji just called. Said you'd given her my number. She wants me to meet her for lunch.'

'Sounds like fun.'

'Yeah, well, I need your help.'

'I've already given you my help.'

'Well, I need more. What if Ji gets upset? What if she cries?' he said darkly. 'That's never good.'

'What? The honourable warrior no good at comforting distraught women?'

'This warrior runs a mile from distraught women,' said Luke. 'I'm amazed you haven't noticed.'

There hadn't been *time* to notice. Not at the pace they'd moved.

'Are you distraught this morning, Maddy?' he asked quietly. 'About what went down last night?'

'Not really. Not exactly. But I am confused so if it's clarity you want from me, Luke Bennett, you're in for disappointment.'

'Clarity's overrated,' he countered. 'I'm sitting here trying to tell myself that I want you to come to lunch simply so you can help with Ji. With my next breath I'm planning how to get you naked with me inside you and to hell with what comes afterwards.'

Not a lot a woman could say to a statement like that.

Not a lot she could do except remember to breathe, and close her eyes tight against the carnality of the visions that assaulted her.

'Maybe we overreacted last night. To the situation at hand,' said Luke, as if he very much wanted to believe it. 'Maybe if we keep our aims and expectations in check this thing between us can work.'

'You mean you're aiming to be here today and gone tomorrow and I'm expected to enjoy it while it lasts and make no demands of you? I know that's what you need from a woman, Luke. I understand why it has to be that way for you. I just don't know if it's going to suit *me*.'

'There's only one way to find out, Madeline,' he said quietly. 'Come to lunch.'

At one thirty-five exactly, Madeline walked into the elegant foyer of the Four Seasons hotel and headed for their high-end restaurant where Peking duck and all the delicate pancake breads and other accompaniments that went with it reigned supreme. She'd booked a table for three under the name of Bennett. According to the floor manager, one of her party already awaited her at the bar. Tentatively, Madeline headed in that direction.

Jianne Xang was everything a Shanghai princess should be. Petite, exquisitely dressed, ethereally beautiful, and intrinsically aloof.

She was also, thought Madeline on closer inspection, incredibly nervous. The eyes did not lie, and Jianne's were fixed, hunted-deer style, on the restaurant door. Madeline's arrival hadn't registered with her. Luke might not have even told her to expect a third person.

If he hadn't, thought Madeline with a sigh of exasperation at the ignorance of men, then Jianne would have discovered at the door that the Bennett booking was a table
for three. No guesses as to whom Jianne expected that
third person to be.

It wasn't until Madeline started towards her that
Jianne's gaze cut to her. Jianne smiled tentatively, polite acknowledgement of a stranger, nothing more, and
then as Madeline kept eye contact Jianne's eyes grew
puzzled.

Madeline had no idea what title to use when greeting
this woman. Mrs Bennett? Possibly not. So she settled for
informality and hoped she would be forgiven the eti-
quette breach.

'Jianne?' she asked, and when the other woman
nodded, 'I'm Madeline Delacourte. Luke asked me to
join you both for lunch. Mind you, it would have helped
had he *mentioned* this to you at some stage.'

'I...see,' said Jianne, only clearly she didn't.

'It'd also help a lot if he were *here*,' said Madeline
dryly. Ji's gaze cut to the door again. Madeline's followed. 'Speak of the devil.'

'You're Luke's...paramour?' asked Ji delicately as he
started towards them.

Nice word, paramour. Courtly and genteel. All the
things her relationship with Luke wasn't. 'Something
like that,' said Madeline. 'It's complicated.'

A hint of sympathy flared deep in Jianne's dark eyes.
'When there's a Bennett involved, it usually is.'

Luke reached them and greeted Jianne with a smile
and a kiss for her cheek before turning towards Madeline.

He did not kiss her cheek, he kissed her mouth, briefly, as if he'd done it a thousand times and would do it a thousand times more before he was through.

'I should have taken one look at you and ran,' she told him wryly. 'I should have listened to your brother.' No point tiptoeing around the subject of Jacob. He might not have been there in person, but he was the *reason* they were there, after all.

Ordering came easy, the Peking duck times three, an extravagant affair that started formal but grew increasingly casual as pancake pockets were filled and different combinations arranged. Even Ji had begun to relax beneath the easy charm of the tiger's golden gaze by the time they were halfway through the meal.

And then, sated, Luke turned to Ji and with typical western bluntness got down to business. 'Your aunt and uncle are worried about you, Ji. They say you need Jake's help.'

Jianne took her time before replying. She finished the morsel of food on her plate and dabbed at her mouth with her napkin before replying.

'They're wrong,' she said. 'I have a slight problem, yes. But I can handle it. There's no need to involve Jake. There was no need to involve any of you, and I apologise for that. My aunt and uncle acted impetuously when they enlisted your help. I should have seen it coming. I should have known they were up to something and put a stop to it.' Jianne shrugged. 'I didn't.'

'So if Jake were to file for divorce, you'd be okay with that?' asked Luke.

Panic flared in Jianne's eyes. Not just an I-think-I've-lost-my-car-keys-panic, but bone-deep fear and anguish. 'Yes,' she said faintly. 'I would be okay with that.'

'And would it help to make your problem go away?' asked Luke more gently.

'That's irrelevant,' said Jianne.

Luke sat back in his chair and his gaze cut to Madeline. What next? he seemed to say.

'Does Jake *want* a divorce?' Madeline asked Luke with a questioning shrug. Heaven knew how, but she seemed to be acting as Jianne's mouthpiece rather than Jacob's. Maybe it was a solidarity-between-women thing.

'Not if it causes Ji problems,' said Luke.

'He's such a sweetheart.' Madeline barely resisted rolling her eyes. Because from where she was sitting, Jake's amenability was more a sign of problem avoidance than active co-operation. 'Would he consider resuming his marriage to Jianne in order to make her problem go away?'

'He's not that sweet,' said Luke dryly.

'Just checking. What if he were to *pretend* to be back in Jianne's life for a time?' Madeline said next. 'Would he do that?'

'He doesn't need to *do* anything,' said Jianne, finally finding her voice. 'That's what I'm trying to tell you. I don't need his help.'

'Better for you, though, if Jacob remains your husband on paper,' said Madeline. 'At least for now.'

'Yes,' said Jianne reluctantly. 'Better for me.'

'Tell Jacob that Jianne doesn't want a divorce,' Madeline told Luke.

'If Jacob wants a divorce he can have one,' said Jianne stubbornly.

'If Jacob had wanted a divorce he'd have gotten one,' countered Madeline. 'Enough with the divorce talk.' Time to find out exactly how big Jianne's problem really was. 'Is this man your father wants you to hook up with a violent man?'

'He's obsessed,' said Jianne quietly. 'He's always been obsessed with me.'

'So you're scared of him,' said Madeline.

'I'm not comfortable around him,' said Jianne. 'I go to a great deal of trouble to ensure that I'm never alone with him.'

'Well, you're scaring me,' murmured Madeline.

'Can't your family do something about him?' asked Luke. 'Like cut him out of your life? I seem to recall your father's had plenty of experience when it comes to turning away people who want to see you.'

Jianne flinched but made no comment.

Madeline shot Luke a warning glance. 'Jianne, why does your father support this man's behaviour?' she asked more gently.

'Guanxi,' said Ji.

'Guanxi?' echoed Luke.

'Indebtedness,' explained Madeline. 'Jianne's father owes this man a favour. Clearly a big one.'

'A daughter is not a *favour.*' Luke's eyes hardened. 'Ji, have you told this man you're not interested in him?'

'Of course I have. In a thousand different ways, including verbally and by letter. Do I look like a mindless puppet to you?' Jianne's eyes flashed.

'Rhetorical question, right?' murmured Luke.

'One of the lessons I learned during my time with your

family was how to stand up for myself. After standing against Jacob I realised I could stand up to anyone.'

Brave words, but Madeline was still mulling over Jianne's comments about having to manoeuvre so as to never be alone with the man. 'What if you asked Jacob along to a couple of events that you knew this man would be at, and then made sure to introduce them, and then left with Jacob, and then maybe stayed the night with Jacob—'

'Maddy,' interrupted Luke with a small negative shake of his head.

'Somewhere big enough that you could have separate rooms—'

'Maddy.' Louder this time.

'So that if this pest followed you he would see that you were well protected and unavailable and go away.' She turned to Luke. 'What? Too complicated?'

'Let's just say I can see a few problem areas,' murmured Luke.

'I see them too,' added Ji. 'Thank you. Really. And thank you for joining me for a meal so we could talk. But I'll be fine.'

Ji set her napkin on the table, retrieved her handbag from beneath her chair, and stood up. 'Please, don't get up,' she added when Luke went to stand. 'Stay and enjoy the rest of the meal.'

Luke stood up anyway. Madeline rose too. She liked Jianne Xang. Liked the other woman's quiet dignity and the way she'd sought to redress the problem and undo her aunt and uncle's machinations.

'If you ever do need help, *call* us,' said Luke. 'Jake can be elusive when it comes to his feelings for you but if you need his protection you'll get it. He owes you that much. We all do. All you have to do is ask.'

'Tiger's left claw,' said Jianne with a gentle smile that spoke of deep and abiding affection. 'It was my name for you, all those years ago. Tristan was the right claw, Hallie was the tiger's ears, and Peter was the tail—always twitching to break free from the rest of you.'

Luke smiled at the fanciful imagery. 'What was Jake?'

'He was the heart.'

CHAPTER EIGHT

MADELINE and Luke continued with the meal once Jianne had gone. One problem had been dealt with but another remained, and Madeline wasn't at all sure how to address it. Easier, far easier, to talk about something else.

'We should have forced a meeting between them,' she said at last. 'It might have done some good.'

'Jake's not ready,' said Luke.

Madeline raised her eyebrow a fraction and gave the tiniest of shrugs. 'So? I wasn't quite ready to see you today either, yet here I am.'

There it was, the opening he needed. 'What do you want to do, Maddy? About us.'

Madeline regarded him solemnly. 'I don't know. I'm trying to decide if I could be your part-time lover. Separate lives, no strings, and no demands. I'm not looking for a husband. I don't need to be kept. In that regard we would suit each other quite well. I just don't know if I can keep my emotions out of the mix the way I've always managed to do before. Not with you.'

'It's okay to care for each other, Maddy. Just not too much.'

'I see.' Maddy shot him one of those are-you-of this-planet looks that women occasionally reserved just for men. 'Define too much.'

'I defined it last night,' he said quietly. 'You can mess with everything but the job.'

That deadly little job.

'So if I were to say to you that we're currently sitting in a restaurant in a very nice hotel and that I'd like to see the inside of a room with you next, would that mess with the job?'

'No, that would mess with my head,' said Luke. Something this woman did with irritating regularity. 'A relationship between us doesn't have to be sordid, Maddy. It just has to be…' What exactly? He searched for a descriptor that would suit.

'Casual and carefree?' she injected dryly. 'Elevator and hotel-room based? Provided, of course, that you're in the country.'

'Fluid,' he said, glaring at her. 'As for our lovemaking being elevator and hotel-room based, it's not as if we're hiding what we're doing. There's no shame in wanting privacy that we can't find elsewhere. It's just…' All he could offer her.

'Practical?' she supplied. 'Neutral territory?'

'Yes.'

Madeline worried at her lower lip for a time and Luke watched her in silence, knowing his offer for a paltry one. Not knowing what he would do should she refuse it.

'Okay, warrior,' she said finally. 'We'll try it your way for a while.' Her eyes met his, guarded and sombre. 'And I'll let you know when I've had enough.'

She was giving him exactly what he wanted by way of a relationship. Her decision should have left him well pleased. Satisfied, even.

It didn't.

A brooding warrior appealed to Madeline almost as much as a reckless one. They left the restaurant and discovered that Jianne had paid for the meal on the way out. They slowed to a halt in the foyer, decision time on what to do with the day and the moment. Madeline looked towards the registration desk. Luke followed her gaze before glancing back towards her as if trying to gauge her thoughts. She let a raised eyebrow speak for her. Luke's lips began to curve.

'This isn't tawdry,' he said.

'Of course not,' she countered. 'It's five-star.'

Luke paid for the room on the way in. Madeline figured she'd have to pay the piper for her recklessness eventually, but not today.

They rode the elevator in silence with another couple. Madeline with her gaze firmly fixed on the floor. This elevator had one of those handy little railings too. The hotel room would have a bed. Madeline had a powerful curiosity when it came to finding out what she and Luke could accomplish given a bed.

The other couple exited the elevator two floors before theirs. Madeline's nerves snapped tight as the lift doors closed. Not here. Don't look at him. Wait.

The elevator doors opened again. Time to get out and walk a while along sterile hotel corridors until they found their room. Madeline hung back a step or two while Luke swiped the access card and opened the door. He stepped back to let her through.

A king-size bed and a high-rise view. A bathroom and a sitting area. A cocoon separating them from the outside world. Not Luke's space or hers. Not the trophy wife and the warrior. Just two people with a need to connect physically for a while. Nothing sordid about it, and if it wasn't quite what she wanted from this man, well, she was used to half measures and compromises when it came to romantic relationships. William had made the most of what she'd given him and never pushed for more. Surely Madeline could do the same when it came to Luke.

Poetic justice, really. The way things turned full circle.

Apprehension and no small measure of lust kicked in hard as Luke shut the door behind him and came to stand in front of her. She set her handbag on the side bench and watched him, curling her hands over the edge of the bench the better to stop them from reaching for him.

His move this time, and she would follow his lead for she didn't know how to play this game of casual lust and hotel-room assignations. She didn't know what to ask for. Didn't know what liberties to take.

'Say something,' he murmured as he slid his hands through her hair, and gently smoothed it away from her face.

'Like what?'

'Say this is okay. What we're doing here. Say you want this.'

'Okay.' She *did* want this. 'I wouldn't be here if I didn't want this.'

Luke's lips came down on hers, teasing and tasting, deepening and always drugging.

Junkie, whispered a little voice deep inside her.

I can handle it, whispered another as Luke's shirt went, and then hers, and then he lifted her onto the side bench, and set his arms either side of her as he put his lips to the hollow of her throat. Madeline tangled her hand in his hair and tilted her head back, willing away everything but the moment. This blindingly perfect moment of craving and capitulation.

Surrender and capture, he served up equal measures of both as he gathered her close, so lost in their lovemaking, so willingly, recklessly lost that there was nothing to do but follow his lead and trust him to know what he was doing.

Junkie, said the voice of doubt, even as his kisses made her tremble. This isn't you. This isn't what you want.

But it was.

The afternoon passed. Neon crept over the city and slid into the room through the gauzy white under-curtains. Luke's need to be inside her had abated somewhat. Madeline's need to have him there had abated somewhat too.

They lay on the sheet-wrecked bed, Luke beside her with one hand on the pillow above his head and his other hand loosely clasping a sheet that rode low on his loins. The tiger was dozing, she thought as she slid across the bed to sit on the edge of it. Magnificent, she thought as she glanced over her shoulder for one more look at him.

Not dozing. Luke's eyes were upon her, heavy lidded and golden, though the rest of him had yet to move a muscle.

'It's getting late,' she said. If they did this again on a weekday she'd have to remember to schedule enough time. Four hours rather than one. 'When did you tell Jake you'd be back?'

'I didn't.'

'Did you tell him you were lunching with Ji?'

'Yes.'

'He'll be waiting to hear from you.'

'I texted him while you ran the shower.' The shower he'd joined her in. Brought her to ecstasy in. Madeline was fast running out of places that didn't hold the memory of him. 'I told him Ji was okay.'

Madeline leaned over and kissed him lightly on the mouth. 'Let me guess, you sent him two words. Four letters. J, I, O, and K. Such compassion.'

'He can hear the rest later,' murmured Luke. 'Ji's in no immediate danger.' Luke reached over and touched the tips of his fingers to the curve of her hip. Surely this insatiable need for Madeline Delacourte would abate soon? It had to, because if it didn't he'd start looking for ways to have more of her. Like basing himself here in Singapore. Like building a life here and making a place for Maddy in it and to hell with his freedom and his wanderlust and his work.

Closing his eyes, Luke shoved those wayward thoughts aside. They weren't useful thoughts. They weren't aims a man in his line of work had any right to consider.

Indulging in just one more taste of Madeline right here and now was a far better goal for a man like him.

Keep it casual. No one gets hurt. It was the only way he knew how to play.

'This going to work for you, Maddy?' he asked quietly.

'Do you hear me complaining?'

'Not what I asked.'

She didn't seem to have an answer to what he asked.

'It seems to be working okay at the moment,' she said with a tiny shrug and a smile that almost reached her eyes.

'Come back to bed,' he said as his fingertips trailed along the underside of her arm and down towards her wrist. 'I'll make it work better.'

Madeline left the hotel later that evening with Luke at her side, her body well satisfied, and her mind awash with magical, sensuous moments. Luke saw her home, declined an invitation to come in for coffee, and told her he'd call her. He didn't say when, and Madeline didn't ask. Keeping it casual, just as he'd asked her to.

She could do this.

Yun had gone to stay overnight with her sister. There were leftovers in the fridge. Madeline ate them in the kitchen, leaning against the counter. Normally, she'd have relished the solitude but tonight she felt restless and the elegantly furnished rooms seemed oddly empty.

No Luke, she thought grimly.

It was enough to send a woman in search of chocolate, and alcohol, and a movie to pass the time. She flicked through the television guide to see what was showing. News, sport, and game shows. Bollywood—no, thank you. Japanese animae was a maybe, with perhaps a little channel surfing and a slice of Hong Kong martial-arts action starring Jet Li on the side.

Hmm. Tough choice. He had a very sweet smile, did Jet Li.

And if warriors were her weakness…and clearly they *were*…why *not* try and substitute one warrior for another?

Ten minutes later, champagne and strawberries at her

side, pillows at her back, and the widescreen remote at her fingertips, Madeline settled to the challenge of forgetting about Luke Bennett for a time. The man wanted a casual relationship. The tiger demanded freedom.

Madeline wanted her mind back.

Jet Li just wanted revenge.

CHAPTER NINE

LUKE'S phone rang in the middle of the night. Not the temporary everyday phone he'd purchased on his way into Singapore. The other phone, the one that rarely rang but when it did he answered the call.

He rolled over, eyes still half closed as he picked up and spoke his name. Voice-recognition software on their end would take care of the rest.

'You know what time it is in Singapore?' he grumbled.

'Yeah, time to rise and shine, princess,' said a smoothly amused voice on the other end of the phone.

Duty called. Luke answered. By the time Luke had all the information he needed he was on his feet, fully alert and reaching for clothes.

He filled his duffel with the tools of his trade and his toiletries and clothes. He checked his toolkits over thoroughly, just in case Po had relocated some of the contents, but everything was in place. The rest of the gear he'd requested would be waiting for him on site.

He needed coffee, he thought as he stripped the bed, replaced the coverlet, and left the sheets in a heap at the end of it. He left his recently purchased dinner suit in the cupboard. He wouldn't be needing it for a while. While he made coffee he wrote Jake a note and called for a taxi to take him to the airport.

A commercial flight would get him to Pakistan. Military transport would take care of the rest.

Luke's mind turned to Madeline. Generous, sensual Madeline who'd given so freely of herself earlier that day. Should he call her? And if he did, what would he say? 'Hey, Maddy. I'm heading out.' And then she'd ask him where, only he had no inclination to tell her. Nowhere pleasant. And then she'd ask for how long, only he couldn't answer that question with any certainty either. One week, maybe two.

He set his duffel by the kitchen doorway and poured the freshly brewed coffee into a mug.

Maybe he could call Maddy's work number and leave a message on her answering machine. He wouldn't have to wake her up at—he glanced at his watch—two thirteen a.m.

Courteous of him.

He wouldn't have to answer any questions.

Smart move.

He wouldn't even have to say goodbye. None of those pregnant pulsing silences that he hated. None of that torturous *be careful* business. As if he planned on being anything else.

Oh, yeah. He liked this plan. He liked it a lot.

Movement in his peripheral vision signalled the presence of another. A small boy who woke at the softest footfall and had yet to sleep for more than a couple of hours at a time.

'You're leaving,' said the boy.

'Yeah. And you should be in bed.'

'Is there a bomb?'

'Something like that.'

'When a bomb explodes when you're trying to dismantle it, you die, right?' said Po.

'Right,' murmured Luke. 'If you don't, chances are you'll wish you had.'

'So you die trying to save people you don't even know?'

'I die with honour.'

Po looked away, but not before the darkness of dissent flashed in his eyes. 'Yeah, but you're still dead.'

Luke fiddled with his cell phone on the way to Changi airport. Vinyl seats and the strong scent of antiseptic assaulted him from within the taxi, the lights of the city skyscrapers bombarded him from outside the car's cocoon. He still hadn't called Maddy. Still hadn't decided on the best tack.

The rational part of his brain was telling him that maybe it wasn't such a bad idea to put a little distance between him and Maddy and an affair that burned just that little bit too hot for comfort. Maybe with distance would come perspective.

The lust-struck part of him simply wanted to hear her voice before he left, but calling her now smacked of a neediness he wasn't ready to admit. Besides, why wake her? The early hours of the morning were never a good time for phone calls. Everyone knew that.

Maybe he'd wait a while before he called her. Tomorrow, her time, so that she'd be alert and awake. That way neither of them would be prone to rash statements made beneath the cover of darkness and with the memory of their recent lovemaking still fresh in their minds. His mind, at any rate.

The abandon with which she'd given herself over to their lovemaking... The way she studied him sometimes, as if she could see straight through him... The way she conducted herself with honour and grit as she moved through a world of high finance and big business; a world as foreign to him as his world was to her. That they'd met and connected at all was a mystery to him, but connect they had and brutal honesty compelled him to admit that if he had his way they'd connect again.

He wasn't done here yet.

He'd call her from Lahore.

Madeline resisted picking up the phone and dialling Luke's number on Monday morning. Casual meant casual. Casual meant that if she hadn't heard from Luke by Wednesday night that she might, *might*, think about giving him a call.

She kept her Monday lunch appointment with Po, though. Nothing else she could do. It was important, this time where Po could speak freely of his new life and raise concerns if he had any. With no disrespect intended towards the many overworked and underpaid social workers who had flitted through Maddy's upbringing, responsibility didn't end with placement. If Po wasn't settling, Maddy wanted to know about it.

But Po had settled beautifully, or so it seemed. It was there in his eyes, and the way he spoke of the sensei. Plenty of hero worship there.

Po's relationship with Luke was far harder to pin down. More complex, and without the structure of sensei and student that Jake had put in place. More turbulent too, judging by the way Po's face darkened when Madeline asked him if he and Luke still trained at night.

'Luke's gone,' said Po abruptly.

Desolation spread through Madeline like a sickness and she clamped down hard on it only to discover that when desolation had been defeated, fear took its place. 'Gone where?'

'Don't know.' Po's bleakness echoed her own. 'He got a phone call last night and left on a job.'

She'd known this would happen. He'd *warned* her, over and over, that this was how it was with his work.

She wanted to quiz the boy. To ask him if he knew any details of the job and whether Luke had said anything about when he'd be back, but it wasn't her place to ask or Po's place to tell her such things so she kept her questions to herself and imagined the worst.

When it came to bombs and the uses people had for them, the worst imaginable could look very bad indeed.

'Luke knows what he's doing,' she said faintly, not sure she could sell this line of reasoning convincingly. Whether Luke knew what he was doing or not, the element of risk was huge. 'He'll be fine.'

She, on the other hand, was fast turning into a wreck. Taking a deep breath, Madeline pictured white clouds wisping across a clear blue sky. The delicate scent of an orange tree in bloom. The faint, fleeting memory of a mother's warm hug all those many years ago. Calmly, Madeline picked up her fork and prepared to eat.

'Do you think he'll come back here?' said Po. 'To Singapore?'

Madeline paused, with a forkful of noodles halfway to her mouth, as calm fled once more, and the roller-coaster ride of emotions began all over again. Hope. Fear. Such a deep and abiding fear of welcoming Luke into her life only to have to live through his death. 'I don't know,' she said raggedly and reached for some more of that elusive inner calm.

Clear skies. Warm water. A lover's gentle—or not so gentle—touch. Thinking calm thoughts really wasn't working for her. 'I guess we'll have to wait and see.'

Luke Bennett returned to Singapore six days later, strung out and dead tired. He'd headed for Singapore instinctively, rather than returning to Darwin, and he figured it for a mistake the minute he walked doggedly into Jake's dojo around seven in the evening—held upright only by the desperate desire to get where he was going before he collapsed.

He'd almost headed for Maddy's—and wouldn't that have gone down a treat? Turning up three days short of a shave and trembling with exhaustion, still reeling from the job and the toll it had taken. Fortunately, a last-minute attack of common sense had prevailed and he'd given the taxi driver Jake's address instead.

He leaned into the doorway, figuring the support would help keep him on his feet a few minutes longer. He looked up and found himself on the receiving end of a shocked and ominous silence.

'What'd I miss?' he asked warily.

Jake looked him over, narrow-eyed and grim. 'What happened to you?'

He should have gone back to Darwin and holed up for a while, the way he usually did. There were too many eyes to deal with here, watching everything he said and did. His gaze slid to the Scotch bottle on the shelf above the kitchen sink.

Wordlessly Jake reached for it, and a glass to go with it, and set them on the table.

Luke slid his duffel to the floor and the room tilted alarmingly.

'Take a seat,' said Jake. It seemed like good advice.

'He's hurt,' said Po.

'I see it,' said Jake. 'What happened to your shoulder?'

'Caught some metal in it.'

'How much metal?' said Jake.

'Nothing a field medic, a pair of tweezers, and a bandage couldn't fix,' rasped Luke, and at his brother's fierce and worried glare, 'It's nothing. A flesh wound. I'm just tired.'

'Po, you want to take his bag to his room?' said Jake.

'There's a duty-free bottle of Scotch in it somewhere,' muttered Luke. 'You might want to leave that with me.'

Po found the Scotch and set it on the table. Still surreptitiously eyeballing Luke, he shouldered the heavy duffel and headed from the room.

Jake waited until the boy had disappeared before continuing with his questions. 'Where'd you go?'

'Afghanistan.'

'Bad?'

'Bad enough. A section of road just full of surprises. Snipers in the hills.'

Jake's gaze cut to Luke's shoulder again.

Luke reached for the Scotch with his good arm and poured a generous measure.

'Any fatalities?'

'No.' The Scotch hit the back of his throat with a satisfying burn. Not this time.

Po skidded back into the kitchen and came to a halt just out of range. Old habits died hard and all that, but it hurt to think that the kid was still so watchful in his presence. Luke didn't know what he expected or wanted from the boy but wary concern wasn't it.

'I put a sheet on the bed,' said Po. 'And a case on the pillow.'

'Thanks, kid.' Luke couldn't be sure if the looking-after of linen was a task Jake had set Po to do or not. He had the sneaking suspicion that, in a way new to formerly homeless street waifs, the boy was trying to mother him. Heaven help him, he didn't want that either.

'You hungry?' said the boy. 'I can read the takeaway menu now.'

'In Chinese and English,' murmured Jake. 'Po's got a brain.'

'There goes the karate,' said Luke, and laughed weakly at Jake's glare. 'Don't order food in on my account, I ate on the plane. And, Po…' He caught the boy's gaze. 'I'm impressed.'

Po beamed and inched a little closer, his gaze following Luke's every move.

More Scotch seemed in order, the fire in it settling ragged nerves and easing the throbbing pain in his shoulder. He'd crash soon. On the narrow little bed with the sheet and the case for the pillow. Not a lot else a man needed. A shower maybe, though he didn't like his chances of staying upright in it. A shower when he woke, then. And then Maddy.

His need to connect again with Maddy hadn't dissipated during his time away. If anything his need for her had grown stronger.

'How's the angel of mercy tracking?' he rasped.

'Maddy's well,' said Jake dryly. 'She dropped by yesterday. I told her we hadn't heard from you. Told her this was normal.'

'It is normal.'

Jake smiled wryly. 'Maybe for you. Her apartment build is going ahead, by the way.'

'Bruce Yi the partner?'

Jake nodded. 'Maddy wanted to let me know that there was no *guanxi* involved. Of course, that didn't stop her from telling me she thought Jianne was heading for a heap of trouble and that I was in the best-placed position to get her out of it.'

'Chances are she's right.' Luke shrugged and his vision blurred as piercing pain shot through his shoulder.

'Anything I should know about that shoulder wound?' said Jake.

'It's clean, I've enough penicillin in me to ward off infection, and I'll need to front at the hospital tomorrow to get the dressing changed. I'm also pretty sure the painkillers are wearing off. There's not a lot else to know.' The wound would heal given time. The bullet had savaged tissue, not bone. 'I gotta sleep.'

Standing took effort. Walking took more. Fully

clothed seemed as good a way to sleep as any. And the bed was just as Po had promised.

Jake watched in silence as Po headed for the doorway and leaned with his back to the frame, presumably watching Luke's progress down the hallway before turning worried eyes to Jake. 'I can stay up tonight,' said the boy. 'I can watch out for him.'

'We both will,' said Jake.

Luke slept hard and dreamless and woke late the following morning. He showered and shaved and instantly felt a million times better. Po and Jake were nowhere about so he headed out the back door and across the road to the noodle bar for breakfast—a huge serve of stir-fried beef that satisfied his hunger, and a scalding-hot coffee laced with condensed milk to temper his thirst. By the time he strode back through the front door of the dojo, he felt almost human.

A class was in progress—Jake heading it and Po a student in it. The kid saw him come in; the kid saw everything. Luke shot him a quick smile and indicated with his head that Po should turn his attention back to the sensei. It was close to ten a.m. Plenty of time for Madeline to have made it to work and settled into the rhythm of her day.

He'd tried calling her from Lahore but he hadn't got through. After that he hadn't been able to call her at all.

The phone call he'd never made and should have made had taken on gigantic proportions. The phone call he was about to make weighed no less heavily on his mind but it was past time he made it.

A secretary answered, asked for his name, and put him on hold. Not an auspicious start.

But Maddy came on the line next and if her words weren't exactly welcoming, at least she deigned to speak with him.

'You're here in Singapore?' she said.

'Yeah.'

'In one piece?'

'More or less.'

'Define less,' she said cautiously.

'Boy, are you suspicious.'

'I prefer to call it smart.'

'I caught a nick to my shoulder,' he offered. 'Nothing to worry about. I just won't be doing push-ups for a while.'

'Really. What else won't you be doing?'

'I've yet to find out.' Luke walked out of the dojo and kept on walking. 'Come out with me,' he said quietly, keeping the need out of his voice, he managed that much, but it was there in the way he gripped his phone and the set of his shoulders.

Madeline hesitated.

Luke felt the world stop.

'Tell me something,' she said a little too steadily for comfort. 'How do you usually take your leave of a woman who's shared your bed? Do you just head off on a job in the middle of the night and never come back? Or do you do her the courtesy of phoning her at some stage to say, hey, I'm out of here but it was fun while it lasted? Or even, hey, I'm heading out but I hope to come back and if I do I'll call you?'

Luke winced. He stopped to lean back against a shop-front wall. 'Okay, so I should have called,' he said gruffly. 'But I shipped out in the early hours of the morning and

I didn't want to call you then. I tried calling you from Lahore but couldn't get through. After that, there was no calling you at all.'

Silence met his words.

'Talk to me, Maddy,' he said raggedly.

'I thought watching you head out on a job would be tough because I'd worry for your safety, and that was part of it, sure enough,' she said. 'But the bit I couldn't cope with at all was not knowing where you and I stood. Whether we were done, or not done. Whether you even planned on returning to Singapore. I can't do that kind of casual, Luke. Not for anyone. It cuts at too many childhood demons. No one ever tells you anything in the foster-care system. You go where you're sent, you start to relax, you start to think that maybe these people are beginning to care for you, just a little. And then one day you wake up and someone wants you gone. No explanations. Nothing. It's as if you'd never existed in the first place.'

'Oh, hell, Maddy. I didn't mean—'

'No. You listen to me and you listen good. It took the unconditional love of a good and kind man before I realised any self-worth whatsoever. It took me years to acquire and I did it one painful step at a time. It took the lack of one early morning phone call from you to shoot a great gaping hole in it. That's something I have to consider when you ring up out of the blue and ask me if I want to see you again. The truth is, I don't know, and it's not just about whether I think I can cope with the demands of your work this time. It's about whether my sense of self-worth is robust enough to dance with you.'

'I'm not gone,' he said, with fear clawing its way up his spine at the thought that she might well be. 'I'm right here. I can't promise I'll always know where we stand, but I can promise to tell you what I do know. I can also be more forthcoming about my movements.' He closed his eyes and let the fatigue he'd thought he'd conquered wash over him. 'I can't fix your reservations about the work I do, Maddy, but I can fix this.'

'Luke—'

'Dance with me.' He could hear the hesitation in her voice. He wanted it gone. 'Come to dinner with me.'

More silence from Madeline's end. Tense silence. 'I've an afternoon full of meetings and I really don't feel like going out tonight,' she said finally.

Hollowness hit Luke hard.

'So here's what I'm offering. Yun's cooking, a quiet night in on my turf, and no promises when it comes to dancing with you. I'm offering you a truce,' she murmured. 'And it's more than you deserve.'

'I accept your offer of truce,' he said. And set about planning for war.

Seven p.m. saw Yun opening the door to Luke with a narrow-eyed glare and a harrumph for good measure. Preparing for war meant wearing clothes he was comfortable in. Clothes Maddy might conceivably want to peel him out of. Well-worn jeans and a button-up shirt he could get out of fast without damaging the shoulder the nurse had put in a sling—the sling he'd worn for half a day and then promptly taken off. A visual reminder of how dangerous his work was definitely wasn't part of this evening's war plan.

A show of strength, a concession offered, and a reminder of the many other benefits of being in his company *was*.

Yun studied him, her gaze lingering on the arm that had already started to ache in the absence of immobility and support. Her own arms stayed firmly crossed. Maybe he held his arm too still and too stiffly, maybe Yun had X-ray vision, but Yun's gaze zeroed in on the exact place the bullet had pierced his skin and refused to budge.

'Tigers should know better than to be seen,' she proclaimed grimly.

'Is Madeline in?' he enquired.

'Yes.'

Nobody moved.

'Can you use fork?' asked Yun.

'Yes.' He was left-handed. His right shoulder had taken the hit. 'I can still use a fork.'

'You could use wrapping for your arm too,' she said. 'But do I see you wearing one? No.' A questioning tilt of finely pencilled eyebrows accompanied her next words. 'I can of course make you one.'

'If you do, could you make it to go?' he said with more than a touch of desperation. 'What say you just sling it over the door handle here and I pick it up on my way out?'

'Why? You think my Madeline won't take one look at you and *know* that you're in pain? She has eyes.'

'Yes, but let's try *not* to draw her attention to that small insignificant detail tonight, okay?'

'Certainly,' said Yun. 'I see your plan and applaud it. You're trying to draw Madeline's attention to your stupidity instead. This should work well.'

Not quite what he had in mind. 'She's in the living room?'

'The small living room. Through the main living room, out through the corridor on the other side, and two doors down on your left. Would you like me to draw you a map?'

'Only if it'll stop you from making a sling. Oh, and here. I picked this up on the way over.' Luke dug in his pocket and withdrew a small plastic sachet containing a selection of mysterious Chinese herbs, spices, and other oddments that probably didn't bear thinking about too closely—everything ground to a very fine powder. 'It's for you. For sweetness. I'm not sure what you're supposed to *do* with it, mind, but the pharmacist swears it'll work.'

Yun took it from him, the tips of her fingers touching the tiniest tip of one corner of the sachet. 'Amateur,' she muttered.

'Have a little faith,' he said as he fished the accompanying business card from his pocket. 'It says here that this particular pharmaceutical company has been in service to three emperors, two foreign queens, and a sultana.'

'And all of them dead.' Yun took the card from him, looked at it, and snorted. 'Would you like me to tell you what it really says?' she enquired ever so sweetly.

'Not sure I need to know. But I'm really glad it's working.'

Smiling, Luke went in search of Madeline. He'd worry about Yun's retaliation—and there *would* be retaliation—later.

Madeline's small living room had just as many bells and whistles as her large one. Massive television screen, state-of-the-art hi-fi and DVD equipment, fabulous furnishings, and eclectic style. Moneyed comfort and elegant sophistication. Madeline's preference. Always.

Easy to enjoy. Not so easy to provide. He didn't need to provide it, Maddy had it already and therein lay one of his dilemmas when it came to being with this woman. The burying of ego and the knowledge that if he did want a more permanent relationship with her then he was going to have to come to terms with stepping into her world as opposed to bringing her into his.

On a superficial level, slotting into Maddy's life and lifestyle wouldn't be difficult for him. He could base anywhere, because his work took him everywhere. Singapore was a transport hub. He even had family here.

On a deeper level, if he based here he would need his own place. Belongings that were his, paid for by him, and if they weren't as luxurious as the ones that surrounded him now so be it. Maybe he and his place and Madeline and her wealth could somehow piece together comfortably for all concerned.

Madeline turned towards him at the sound of his footfall. She looked comfortable and carefree, her delectable body clad in faded jeans and a dove-grey T-shirt, her honey-streaked hair caught up in a loose ponytail. He wanted to reach for her, as if it were his right only he knew it wasn't so he stayed his hand and looked his fill instead.

'Greetings, warrior,' she said wryly. 'It's good to see you. Alive.'

Direct hit and best glossed over. 'You're looking very fine too.'

'Thank you.' He thought he saw the hint of a blush colour her cheeks as she turned away and reached for the television remote and flicked through the channels. He ached to loosen her hair and run his fingers through it, bury his face in it, before claiming her lips with his own. He'd done all that and more during the afternoon they'd spent at the hotel but that was then and this was now. Foolish to think that they could simply pick up where they'd left off with no adjustments, no matter how much he wanted to. The world simply didn't work that way.

'Your brother called,' said Madeline next.

'What did he want?'

'To tell me to either send you home early or keep you overnight. He seems to think you're a little knocked around.' She turned her head and surveyed him critically from top to toe. 'I think he's right.'

'Maddy, not you too,' said Luke quietly. 'Between Jake and Po today, I've had just about all the mothering I can take.'

'Poor baby. Then again you will go and get yourself shot…'

So much for keeping that little titbit to himself.

Yun shuffled into the room bearing a silver tray upon which sat a crystal tumbler of amber liquid that he really hoped was Scotch. The diminutive housekeeper halted beside Luke's elbow and eyed him sternly.

'If this is your idea of informal I'd hate to be here on a regular night,' he told her.

'Drink,' said Yun.

'What is it?' Too many twigs in it for it to be Scotch. Return fire came fast around here.

'Good for you,' said Yun. 'Drink.'

Luke liberated the glass from the tray in the hope that Yun would then go away. She didn't. He looked to Maddy for support.

'Drink,' said Maddy.

'You first,' he said, holding out the glass to her.

'What? You think I'm trying to poison you?' Madeline took the glass from his hand and sipped. 'Jake told me about your sister's funeral vase experience, by the way. Fascinating.'

Luke retrieved the glass and downed the contents. Swallow, swallow, crunch and swallow. So his imagination had led him ever so slightly astray. It wasn't as if he'd ever really *believed* it.

Yun left. Madeline smirked.

Luke figured that as long as he was being tarred with the stupid brush he might as well go all out to deserve the coating. 'May I ask a delicate question?'

'If you must.'

Luke eyed the various surfaces and ledges in the room. 'Where's William?'

'In the family crypt at the cemetery. Where else would he be?'

'Oh, I don't know...' murmured Luke. He could have sworn Yun had just fed him a bird's nest. 'Here?'

'How *do* you keep that imagination of yours in check?' she asked.

'Practice.'

The food came out. Yun set it out, smorgasbord-style along a sideboard. A lot of food for two people, unless Maddy had an appetite he didn't know about or another half a dozen people were coming to dinner. 'You're expecting more company?' he queried.

Madeline followed his gaze and a smirk crossed her lips. 'No.'

'Eating for three?'

'Let's hope not,' she murmured, 'for I really can't see that fitting in with your plans or mine any time soon.'

'How about in the somewhat distant future?' he said. 'Would children factor into your plans then?'

'I really haven't thought about it.'

'Did they factor into your plans with William?'

'No,' she said after a moment's hesitation. 'And it wasn't because of William's age or because I didn't care for him enough to go down that road. William was sterile. He was quite resigned to life without progeny. As for me, I figured if any latent maternal instincts did kick in I could help existing unwanted children towards a better life instead.'

'So…they did kick in,' said Luke carefully. 'Your maternal instincts.'

Madeline smiled. 'Stand easy, warrior. I've no plans to trap you into fatherhood. You're not a good bet.'

He knew he wasn't, not with the lifestyle he currently led, but her casual dismissal of his potential to be a good father at some stage stung nonetheless. Luke turned his attention to the food and tried to put the notion that Madeline thought him a bad fatherhood bet behind him. She was right. The way his life was structured now didn't encourage strong ties of any kind.

The question now being how much was he prepared to change that lifestyle in order to accommodate the formation of such ties?

Not fatherhood ties. Not that. But other less alarming ties. Still strong, mind. Just not the superglue variety. 'I've been thinking about what you said on the phone,' he said. 'About what you need from a relationship and what I can supply. I have a few ideas.'

She looked wary. Vulnerable. He knew the feeling.

'I had it in mind to answer any questions you might want to ask me about my work,' he offered. 'I figure the more you know, the less likely you'll be to worry for my safety.'

Maddy's eyes cut to his shoulder. 'Why do I get the feeling that this is a concession you don't often make?'

'Because you're smart?' Fact was, he'd never made such a concession before. He'd never talked about his work to anyone, and that included his brothers. He rubbed his neck with his good hand to cover his sudden nervousness.

'All right,' she said guardedly. 'First question. Are you ever contactable when you disappear on these jobs? As in if I needed to contact you is there a number I can call?'

Not such a hard question to answer. 'Often I'm contactable on my mobile right up until I enter the hot zone. Once I'm in the zone, contact ceases. There are numbers I can give you in case of an emergency.'

'How long are you usually in this hot zone?'

'It varies. A lot of time I spend away is taken up with travelling. Then there's planning, paperwork, and rest. On a routine disarm, hot-zone time is minimal. I usually know exactly what weapon I'm dealing with and what I have to do. I go in, I do the job, and I get out. I'm talking minutes rather than hours.'

Madeline smiled wryly. 'You make it sound so easy.'

'I'm very fond of easy,' he said. 'But in the interests of full disclosure there will occasionally be times when you won't be able to contact me for weeks. On those jobs I'll be part of a military operation. Communication is limited because we're in unsecured territory. War zones and the like. Those jobs are few and far between but they do exist.'

'Was your last job one of them?'

'Yes.'

Madeline's gaze cut to his shoulder again. 'Full disclosure really isn't helping your cause,' she murmured.

'Yes, but next time I go away if I can tell you it's a routine pass over an armed missile chances are you won't worry.'

'That's really not how worry works,' she said dryly. 'Although I do sincerely appreciate your efforts to set my mind at ease.'

'It gets easier, Maddy.'

'Really? How would you know?' Amusement laced with bite and he was ridiculously glad of it. He far preferred the confident, smart-mouthed Madeline to the fragile waif he so didn't want to break.

'Okay, so I've *heard* it gets easier. Long-term Navy wives *swear* they hardly worry about their husbands at *all*.'

'Have you ever stopped to wonder *why*?'

'Resilience,' said Luke.

'Indifference,' countered Madeline.

'Cynic.'

'Idealist,' she shot back.

'I missed you,' he said.

Madeline shook her head and looked away from the beautiful warrior who was Luke Bennett. Shattering her defences one by one. Methodically. Deliberately. Until he'd stripped her raw. 'Have you any idea how hard it is for me to take a chance on you, Luke Bennett?'

'I have a fair idea,' he said quietly.

'My father self-destructed. So did my brother. Both of them chasing death and there was nothing I could do to stop them.'

'I'm not like them, Maddy.'

'No?'

'No.' Luke's gaze met hers, blazing gold and fiercely implacable. 'I don't court death. I hate it. I do everything in my power to ensure it doesn't claim innocent lives. I do my damnedest to make sure that it doesn't claim me. I protect the things I love, Madeline. I don't abandon them.'

Madeline blinked away the sting of tears and drew a deep breath as Yun came in to clear the remains of the meal away. Madeline watched as the old housekeeper's eyes widened momentarily at the amount of food they'd managed to consume. A smile threatened to crack open Yun's timeworn face. Luke saw it too. He didn't miss much, this lovely defiant warrior. And when he found a crack he instantly pressed his advantage.

'Thanks, Yun,' he murmured, and began to stack the plates nearest to him. Yun stopped him with a not so gentle smack to his forearm. Madeline smirked.

'Rest arm,' snapped Yun. 'Fool. Less and less like tiger, more and more like ox.'

'Strong?' prompted Luke. 'Steadfast?'

'Stubborn,' corrected Yun.

Luke pointed to an empty dish. 'What was this one?'

'BBQ duck with sweet sauce, red chilli, and ginger,' said Yun. 'You like?'

'Definitely.'

'For strength,' Yun muttered and stalked away.

Once all the food had disappeared and Yun along with it, Madeline's apprehension about what to do about Luke Bennett grew. 'Would you like to come through to the lounge area?' she said awkwardly. 'It might be more comfortable for your arm.'

'The arm's fine,' he said steadily, but he headed for the soft suede lounge and leaned back into it as Madeline fiddled with the channels again and, lacking anything suitable, finally switched over to music. William had loved classical music and in time Madeline had come to love it too. All the different colours and hues of emotion that mankind had yet to find words for. Today's colour was blue. Soothing, she hoped. A little slice of calm in a world made ever more complicated by a pair of warm golden eyes.

'Nice,' he murmured.

'Really?'

'Really,' he said and watched her while she hovered by the entertainment system. Madeline stayed where she was, caught as she was between wanting to sit next to him on the sofa and knowing that if she did go and sit by him, and allow herself to touch him, she'd be lost and they'd be right back where they were before he went away.

'I've been thinking about basing myself here in Singapore,' said Luke, his murmured words wrapping around her like a silken thread. Simultaneously beautiful and terrifying. She didn't speak. She couldn't breathe. More than she'd hoped for. Far more than she dared take.

'It'd mean I'd be here in between jobs. Not at the dojo. I'd find a place of my own.'

'You'd need residency,' she said, trying to sound non-committal, as if where he decided to base himself was neither here nor there to her. 'And a job.'

'I have a job.'

'A job that benefits Singapore's economy or its people.'

'You don't think they'd see my job in that light?'

'I don't know what they'd think,' she said, brutally honest. 'But I think if you're really serious about this you might want to bypass the immigration clerks in favour of someone with a little more clout. Letters of reference wouldn't hurt either.'

'Noted,' he said. 'I'm looking at residency here for a number of reasons. Being closer to family is one of them.'

'Family's important,' she murmured. It was a good reason for him to be thinking about relocating to Singapore in between jobs. She couldn't fault it.

'That Singapore is a major transport hub doesn't hurt either.' He looked so relaxed. So at ease, sitting there on her lounge. So far his reasoning was entirely logical. Maybe he wasn't looking to deepen their relationship. Maybe he was simply rearranging his closet.

'And then there's you.'

Madeline's heart thudded in her chest. Hope. Fear. Each of them fighting for supremacy.

'I'm not trying to pressure you into a relationship you're not interested in pursuing, Madeline, but you said on the phone that you wanted to know where we stood. That you needed a statement of intent from me, so here it is. I want to explore this thing between us, Maddy. I'm willing to give it the time it deserves and I want to see what comes of it. This is my intent.'

'You'd really rearrange your life so there was room for me in it?' she asked raggedly. She always had been a sucker for being wanted. *One day when I'm older… One day when I'm out of the system… One day when someone wants me…*

'It's not such a big deal, Maddy. Changing home base isn't as big a hassle for me as it is for some. I'd still only be here a couple of weeks out of every five. And I live light. I don't have all the accompaniments a lot of people have—'

'Luke,' she interrupted. 'Shush. You're spoiling my moment. I'd like to enjoy it just a little longer if you don't mind.'

A slow smile stole across his face. Sunshine after rain. 'So…you like the idea?'

She still had to think through all of the ramifications, but, yes. 'Let's just say it's growing on me.' She went to him then, and straddled him, mindful of his arm but not careful of his mind as she leaned into him for a slow and gentle kiss that a woman might wish would never end. 'You make it sound so simple.'

'It is simple. Easy, even.' He urged her forward and into another languid kiss. Slow and savouring and heart-breakingly perfect. 'I'm very fond of easy.'

'Welcome to Singapore,' she whispered.

He stayed the night. And he took Maddy easy.

Waking the next morning and leaving her bed with a naked Luke Bennett in it proved something of a challenge for Madeline. But he'd loved her thoroughly during the night and he slept deeply now and Maddy had no wish to wake him. Better for her to shower and get ready for work and for Luke to sleep and let his body mend and wake at will. She didn't like the chances of Luke's shoulder getting much rest while he was awake.

Maddy surveyed the square gauze bandage taped to his skin between collarbone and shoulder with a furrowed brow. The bandage was the size of her hand and the faint stain of dried blood darkened the gauze. Madeline hated the stark reminder that Luke wasn't infallible and that he could be hurt.

Don't mess with the job, he'd told her, and had then proceeded to outline how he worked, so that she would have a better understanding of it. She appreciated the gesture, she really did. Whether it would help her cope better the next time he went away remained to be seen. She'd try, though—he'd won that much concession from her.

She had the disquieting feeling that Luke Bennett could convince her to try just about anything.

CHAPTER TEN

LUKE woke slowly, wincing as he rolled onto his side and remembered his shoulder injury first, and where he was second. Madeline's bed, only Maddy wasn't in it. The bedside clock read ten past eleven, which gave him a clue as to why he was alone. Madeline would be at work.

He leaned over the side of the bed and found his phone in the pile of clothes on the floor.

'You left without saying goodbye,' he said when finally he reached her.

'So did you.'

Ouch. 'Wake me next time,' he muttered. 'Because the next time a job comes calling I fully intend waking you.'

'Appreciated,' she said smoothly.

'I'm still at your place.' He needed a shower but figured for courtesy's sake that he could make do without until he got to Jake's. 'How do I get *out* of your place without encountering the tiny terror?'

'You don't,' said Madeline. 'Yun fully intends feeding you before you go. I left her poring over cookbooks relating to the care and feeding of wounded warriors.'

'They've got cookbooks for that?'

'Oh, yes. Some of them date back dynasties. I hope you like gruel.'

'She really doesn't need to make a fuss,' said Luke a touch desperately.

'Oh, there'll be no fuss.' Madeline's smile transmitted down the phone line loud and clear. 'I have to go. I've a meeting about to begin, but I'm glad you slept soundly and I hope you're feeling a little better this morning. Is that too much mothering for you?'

Decidedly not. If anything it felt a little light. 'You could always swing by the dojo on your way home from work,' he murmured, and hoped he didn't sound as needy as he felt. 'There's a vacant apartment a couple of blocks east that I want to take a look at. It belongs to Mr Chin who runs the takeaway across the road from Jake's.'

'You'd take a rental contract before you got permission to stay in Singapore?' asked Madeline. 'That's pretty bold, warrior. Reckless, even.'

'Chin's willing to rent it by the month while I can get that sorted. I prefer to call it forward thinking and seeing as Delacourte is heavily invested in the rental market hereabouts I figured your opinion on location and price might be well worth listening to.'

'Opportunist,' she said.

'So you'll come and look at it with me?'

'Of course. I'll pull up some figures for you today. Also some Delacourte options, if you're interested. Is it furnished?'

'No.'

'You do believe doing things the hard way,' she said on a sigh.

'There are shops in Singapore,' he countered. 'Buy a bed, a fridge, and a table, and if I don't get residency I'll give them to Jake. And, Maddy, about those Delacourte options… I appreciate your offer. I really do. But becoming your tenant is about on par with having you pick me up in your car. It's a beautiful ride but it rubs.'

'Your call,' she said coolly.

'It is.' And a big call it was too, for a man lying stark naked in her bed and about to be fed gruel by her maid. 'You've got your issues, Maddy. I've got mine. We just need to give them a bit of space to be, that's all.'

'All right,' she said in a voice carefully stripped of emotion. She still didn't like it, he thought, but she wore it, because he'd asked her to. 'I'll meet you at seven this evening and we'll look at the apartment and after that you can take me to dinner as payment for my expertise. How does that sound?'

'Perfect,' said Luke. 'Now, are you sure there's no way out of here without going past Yun?'

'Not unless you're related to Superman and can fly,' she said dryly. 'Prepare to be fed, warrior. Yun likes to cook for people who like to eat. I saw what you ate last night. I have faith in your ability to please.'

'Enjoy your meeting, Delacourte,' he said. 'Go make business grow.'

'I'm glad you thought of me when you woke,' she said after a pause. 'I'm glad you called me. You made my day.'

Then she hung up.

Two weeks passed by in a blur of project work for Madeline and a crash course in home furnishings for

Luke. His tables and chairs were old and mismatched, some of the chairs from Jake's and some of them from Chin's restaurant. No wardrobes to speak of, a new fridge and a new bed.

It turned out that Luke enjoyed wielding a hammer, and with Po's assistance and the acquisition of half a dozen old wooden pallets they'd knocked up a bookshelf and two bedside tables. They'd started on another book-shelf build after that—this one for the sensei. Next on the list was a desk. Luke had gone to great lengths to secure some exquisitely grained antique hardwood for the job. The desk was for Po.

Luke's collection of power tools grew and so did Maddy's amusement, for the man still hadn't got around to purchasing cutlery or cookware and stared at her blankly when at last she suggested it.

Each to his own.

Po became, if not a fixture at Luke's apartment, then at least a regular visitor. Madeline became a regular visi-tor too, revelling in Luke's casual acceptance of her ap-pearing without notice and the not so casual lovemaking that often came afterwards.

This night, though, Madeline had received instruc-tions from Yun to bring the tiger if she must but to get herself home and plan to stay home for the rest of the evening, because Yun had been cooking, and someone sure as hell needed to eat it.

Madeline had winced guiltily at Yun's pointed com-ment. She'd kept up with her work these past two weeks, and she'd kept up with Luke and with Po. The person she hadn't kept in mind and in her heart was Yun.

'I have a dinner invitation for you,' she said when she meandered into Luke's apartment that evening. The man had acquired a café-sized coffee-making machine between last night and this one. He'd probably scrounged it from Chin's and it probably didn't work because pieces of it were scattered across the kitchen bench. 'My place, tonight. I'm heading there now, Yun's been cooking, and you're welcome to stay over.'

'Fine,' he said cheerfully. 'Want me to bring anything?'

'Charm,' said Madeline. 'Yun's feeling neglected.'

'I'll get some on the way,' he said. 'I know this place.'

Yun opened the door to Luke that evening with a narrow-eyed glare. Luke took one look at her, dug his peace offering from his pocket and handed it to her without preamble. 'Charm,' he said. 'Enjoy.'

Whatever she was cooking smelled absolutely fantastic. Within half an hour the sideboard in the informal living room was groaning beneath the weight of the delicacies being thrust upon it.

'First course,' said Yun, only this time Luke followed the tiny terror back to the kitchen.

He studied the benches and the abundance of food set out on them in various stages of preparation. Yun must have been working all day on this, or more. Not one of these dishes looked simple. Every last one of them smelled divine.

Madeline stepped into the kitchen, her eyes widening as she took in the spread.

Yun stood there defiant. Madeline's lips twitched. 'I hope you're hungry,' said Madeline.

'I hope you're joking,' he said. 'We're going to need more people.'

So Madeline got on the phone and invited Jake and Po to join them and the old housekeeper's eyes gleamed.

The Bennett clan, of which Po was now a member, worked their way steadily and with great enjoyment through Yun's feast. Yun lost her sternness, started to smile, and she positively beamed when at the end of the meal Po opted into the clean-up process, ruthlessly efficient and very, very swift.

After that evening the balance of the relationship changed subtly.

Luke, getting the hint that Yun enjoyed company, and stopping by Madeline's more regularly rather than waiting for her to come to him, often with Po in tow, sometimes when Madeline was there and sometimes not.

Madeline returning home late from work one night to find Luke, Jake and Po learning t'ai chi from Yun up on the rooftop garden. Hard for her not to savour each golden moment of this makeshift family that was so much more than she'd ever had.

Luke, watching the images that rolled through Madeline's digital photo frame.

'That's Remy,' she told Luke willingly enough one evening. 'My brother.' Gaunt-faced and drug-addled. Hell-bent.

The next picture came up. An older man standing with Remy at the bow of a boat. 'William,' she said, and brought her knees to her chest and wrapped her arms around them. Luke rarely asked her about her life with William but it sat there between them at times, an elephant in the room. 'He was the one who helped me get Remy out of Thailand and back here to Singapore and into hospital. He hardly knew us, he *didn't* know us, but he stopped, and he saw, and he helped us.'

The next photo appeared. A picture of William and herself dressed for a ball. She looked very young. William looked every bit his age.

'Why?' said Luke. Same question he'd always asked and one she'd never been able to answer to his satisfaction.

'Because he was there for me,' she offered finally. 'Because sometimes a person's past isn't pretty, and sometimes out of the darkness something good comes along and you never forget it. Remy was my nightmare. William was my something good.'

Luke closed his eyes and ran his fingers through his hair. 'God, Maddy,' he said raggedly.

'I know you don't understand why I married him.' She didn't care what society at large thought of her marriage to William, but she'd come to care a great deal about what this man thought. 'But it wasn't for his money and it wasn't out of gratitude. It was because he saw me as I was. Driven, hungry, desperate, and in spite of all that he loved me anyway. I'd never had that. I craved it.' She rested her chin on her knees and willed Luke to look at her and finally he did. 'So I took it.

'I don't regret it,' she said when Luke remained silent. 'I will always honour William and the time I spent with him. In the way I run Delacourte. In the respect I have for myself today. I hope you can understand that.'

'I do,' he muttered and gathered her close, knees and all, warming her with his nearness as he brushed the backs of his fingers against her cheek. 'I do understand. I just wish…that someone had protected you more, *cared* for you more, when you were younger. Maybe if they had you wouldn't have made the choices you did.'

'Please don't paint me the victim, Luke.' She stared at him through troubled eyes. 'If you do, I'll only disappoint you. You need to understand that marrying William was a choice I made of my own free will. I'm not a victim. I never have been, and I can't play that role. Not even for you.'

'I'm not asking you to.'

She wanted to believe him. She badly wanted to believe that he saw her, all of her, and accepted her for the person she was. Damaged. Driven. And devoted, in her way, to the memory of a man who had given her so much and asked for so little. 'I never loved him, Luke.' Not the way she could come to love this man if she let herself. 'I told you that once before and you didn't like it. You still don't like it and there's nothing I can do or say to change that. But honour William…that I can do.'

Luke closed his eyes, blocking her out, as if refusing to see the parts of her he didn't want to see. 'I understand honour,' he said gruffly.

'I know you do.'

'And I'm doing my damnedest to understand you. It's not easy for me, Maddy. You tear me apart sometimes.'

'I know that too.'

Another week passed and Luke and Po built a study desk befitting an industry lion. Po's job now was to sand the desk down, and he spent most of his evenings at Luke's place, working his way through the various grades of sandpaper until the wood felt as smooth to the touch as polished marble.

'You need to think about what kind of stain or polish you want on it,' said Luke as Madeline looked on from the doorway, coffee cup in hand. She'd come straight from work and she couldn't stay long for a charity meeting beckoned, but even a quick fix was better than nothing these days.

'Can I keep it this colour?' asked Po.

'You can do anything you want,' said Luke. 'Although you might want to put some sort of sealant on it to protect the wood. Doesn't have to be paint—we could probably use oils and wax and I reckon I know who'd have a recipe.'

'Yun,' said Po. 'I'll go see her tomorrow.'

'It might make the wood look a little bit darker,' said Madeline. 'Richer in colour. Deeper.'

'That'd be all right.' Po put the sandpaper down and started wiping the desk over with a square of black silk Luke had picked up from somewhere. Small boy, dark, wary eyes that saw everything and revealed little. 'Luke...' said the boy hesitantly. 'You know how you just said I can do anything I want...'

Luke stopped rolling up the extension cord and gave the boy his full attention.

'Do you think the sensei would mind if I didn't become a martial arts master?'

'I thought you liked martial arts training.'

'I do,' said Po earnestly. 'And I still want to do it every day and every night. But I want to be something else when I grow up.'

'What do you want to be?' said Luke.

'A lawyer.'

To his credit, Luke didn't point out the obvious. That law required education and Po had so far refused to even consider giving them the information they needed to get him enrolled in a school.

'I don't think Jake would mind,' said Luke.

'A human rights lawyer,' said Po next.

Luke smiled a little at that. 'I don't think Jake would mind at all.'

And then the phone that usually sat silently on Luke's nightstand rang and Luke froze. Maddy watched him expectantly, and when he didn't make a move to pick up the call, she felt the ghost of trepidation skid down her spine.

Luke's gaze cut to hers, storm-tossed and wary.

'Phone,' she said, and knew what was coming. Within a few hours the fabric of her world would rip and remake itself once again and Luke would be gone.

No, thought Luke when he first heard the phone ring. Not now. That life had nothing to do with the life he enjoyed now.

Only it did.

He didn't need a regular job on account of the work he chose to do. Then there was the not so small matter of the adrenalin junkie in him flat out enjoying a life-or-death challenge. It was only the fear of how the call would affect Madeline that stayed his hand.

'You want me to get that?' she said.

'No.' Breathing deeply, Luke strode from the room

and took the call. He headed for the window, looking out unseeingly over the now familiar streetscape as he went through the motions, and got the details he needed to get. Game on.

Maddy and Po stood together as a unit when, finally, he turned around.

'That was work,' he said, but by the looks on their faces they'd already figured that out. 'They've found a World War Two sub in deep water west of Guam. It's intact and it's armed. They need divers.' He looked to Madeline. 'Like me.'

Madeline bit her lip and looked away. 'When do you leave?'

'A flight leaves for Guam in three hours.'

'Handy,' she said.

'Don't go,' said Po. Small boy, fists clenched as he stood there, eyes burning. 'Why do you have to go? Nobody needs saving this time. Everyone's already dead.'

'Po,' said Maddy softly, before Luke could speak. A tiny shake of her head accompanied her words. 'Don't.'

The boy's eyes filled with tears as he whirled around and hightailed it from the room and then the apartment. Back to Jake's, Luke could only hope. Jake, who offered stability and structure and learning. All the things that Luke couldn't.

Barricading his heart against the pain of Po's desertion, Luke turned his attention back to Madeline. This was why a man in his position never messed with other people's lives. This was why he should have stayed away from Maddy and from Po. 'Are you going to tell me I'm insane for doing what I do too?'

She smiled slightly, but her eyes remained sad. 'No.' And when he didn't reply, 'I know what you are, Luke Bennett. A warrior born, who will *never* ignore a call to arms. Honour demands it, the tiger wants it, and you told me what to expect. My memory's not that bad.' She whirled away, unable to hold his gaze. 'Do you know how long you'll be away?'

'No,' he admitted. 'A week or two, maybe more. Depends how many torpedoes there are on board.' Maddy shuddered and Luke shut his mouth fast. Too much information. He crossed to his laptop case and rummaged through the pockets for the piece of paper he was looking for. 'I said I'd leave you a list of emergency contact names and numbers.' He grabbed a pen and put an asterisk beside one particular name and number before handing the paper to her.

She looked at the numbers and her lips twisted briefly. 'Thanks.'

'I'll be staying on board an American frigate. Chances are I will be able to get messages through to you. There'll be down time between dives. A lot of it.'

'Thanks again.' Her shoulders squared as she took a deep breath and turned to face him. Her smile was bold, but her eyes destroyed him.

'Maddy, I need my head in the game,' he muttered desperately.

'I know.' Madeline set her coffee mug carefully on the bench and leaned against the doorframe because she knew her strength was fading and that if Luke didn't leave soon her words would echo Po's. 'Go,' she said softly. 'Be safe. Don't think of me. And I won't think of you.'

He took her lips in a kiss she would remember for ever. Ravenous and worshipping, he broke her in that moment.

'I'm coming back,' he whispered, and Madeline closed her eyes against the devastating impact of those words coming from this man.

'You don't know that.'

'Pessimist.'

'No, just a realist.'

'Believe in me, Maddy. Please.'

'I do.' She opened her eyes, straightened her spine and headed for the door. Walk, she told herself. You've said goodbye and you've given him your blessing so keep walking, Madeline, and don't you dare look back.

If she did she would beg him to stay.

Madeline found Jake in his office. Po wasn't with him. 'Have you seen Po?' she said.

'He just went by on his way out the back. I thought he'd forgotten something and had come back to grab it.' Jake eyed her searchingly 'Trouble?'

'A job came in for Luke,' she muttered.

'Ah.' Jake's clear blue gaze turned oddly sympathetic. 'How would you like to learn karate?'

'Does it relieve stress, release aggression, and render the body exhausted?' she said.

'Got it in one.'

'I'll think about it,' she said. Right now her mind was far too awash with other chaotic emotions. 'I think I may have a slight problem,' she said.

'Feel free *not* to share,' said Jake.

'I think I've fallen in love with your brother.' Oh, yes. The words felt comfortable on her tongue. Love had finally arrived in Maddy's universe and it was every bit as terrifying as she'd thought it would be. 'Even if he is a clueless, thrill-seeking danger-loving imbecile.'

'Please tell me you're not confiding in me.' Jacob looked desperate. Beyond desperate and heading straight for panic. 'I don't deserve this. I really don't.'

'Po is *very* upset,' she continued acidly.

'Uh-huh.' Jake lit out of his chair and headed for the back rooms. Madeline followed.

'He thinks Luke is going to get himself killed.'

'Uh-huh.' Jake hit the kitchen and headed for the shelf above the sink. The Scotch came down and two mis-matched juice glasses appeared. Jake clearly paid the same attention to kitchenware as his brother. He had a very generous pouring hand, though.

'Drink this,' he said, and shoved an almost full glass in her hand.

Madeline drank, gasping at the liquid's fiery burn. 'I mean, what if he does die? What then? How are the people he left behind going to feel?' Madeline downed another mouthful of Scotch. She knew exactly how they'd feel. She had all the experience in the world when it came to the death of loved ones. Her mother. Her father. Her brother. Then William. She was a veritable death *magnet*.

'Try grateful,' said Jake. 'For having known him and loved him.'

'So much for sympathy.'

'You have my sympathy, Madeline. You do,' he said

gruffly. 'But I'm proud of my brother—of the man he is and the work he does. You want me to tell you what he got his last Victoria Cross for? A five-year-old Cambodian girl and her big brother had gone into a mine-field looking for metal scrap. Luke and his operations team were working the next minefield along when they heard the explosion. The girl's brother died instantly. The little girl sat down and waited for someone like Luke to come along.'

Maddy stood immobile, stuck in the scene Jake had painted for her—sitting right there next to that little girl.

'Would you have had him say no?' asked Jake. 'Would you have had him say he couldn't go and get her because there were people at home who he loved and who loved him and that he couldn't risk his life for fear of hurting them?'

'No,' said Madeline and swallowed another belt of Scotch. 'No, I'm glad he went and got her.'

'This work of Luke's that you so object to…it's not just something he does for kicks,' said Jake. 'It's what he is, and it runs soul deep, so if you can't respect his decision to put himself on the line, again and again, and love him all the more for it, I suggest you get out of his life.'

Brutally blunt. A blazing blue-eyed warrior who guarded his departing brother's back.

'You going to hurt my brother, Maddy?' said Jake. 'Or do you love him enough to stay?'

Maddy clenched her fist and searched her heart for the courage required of a warrior's woman. 'What do the people who stay behind and wait usually do to pass the time?' she asked.

Jake's glance slid towards her nearly empty Scotch glass.

'Besides drink,' she said with a choking laugh.

Fifteen minutes later, three shadowy figures stood in a dojo practice hall and began to move slowly through the forms.

CHAPTER ELEVEN

Luke Bennett had never been one to lose focus while on the job. American patrol vessel, same old game—with Luke the on-call expert and the US Navy calling the shots. Dive-team rotations, twenty-four seven, until the last of the torpedoes had been disarmed and secured. On-deck demonstrations, showing dive teams how to pull those Japanese torpedoes apart without making big waves. Riding shotgun underwater as a young marine disarmed his first banger. He did his job and he did it well.

And in between all that he experienced something he'd only ever encountered once before, way back when his mother had died.

Emptiness, and with it an increasing uncertainty over what he might find upon his return.

Would Po, who didn't understand why Luke did what he did, still want to work on the desk? Would Yun cook enough food for an army upon his return or would she too withdraw her support?

He wondered if Madeline would work late and catch up on work she'd been neglecting. The apartment-block build and the thousand other tasks and decisions that came of running a business empire. He wondered if their relationship was solid enough to withstand his time away or whether upon his return Madeline would finally tell him she'd had enough.

He tried reading books.

He tried kicking round the gym.

He tried killing time with his fellow divers. Hand-reel fishing and cracking golf balls off the stern, along with bad jokes and tall stories of twenty-foot white sharks and sirens both real and imaginary. Those things that would usually go some way towards entertaining him.

He tried calling her. A communications officer at his side, dialling him out and telling him he had three minutes.

She picked up on the third ring.

'Maddy.'

'Where are you?' she said.

'Still working,' he told her. 'Still shipside.'

'So, the job's going well?' she asked warily. 'Are you okay?'

'Fine,' he said. 'I'm fine. The job's fairly routine. I just had a window in which to call you, that was all, so I did.' He was no good at this. He had no practice at long-distance small talk. 'How are things with you?'

'Good,' she said. 'Good.' And lapsed into a silence he didn't know how to fill.

'Po's been making something for you out of the table offcuts,' she said finally. 'I don't want to spoil the surprise but it's beautiful. I think it's an apology of sorts for lashing out about your work.'

'He doesn't need to apologise,' muttered Luke.

'Yes,' said Madeline. 'He does.'

More awkward silence, while his three minutes ticked away.

'How's Jake?' he said. Small talk, because any other kind of talk would undo him.

'Jake's well.'

'And you?' He'd already asked her that. Fool.

'I'm well too. Working hard. Keeping busy. Coping.'

'Good,' he said. 'Good.' While a small part of him wished that she didn't sound quite so together and that his absence had left a gap she couldn't fill. 'There's another week or so's worth of work here. I'll call when we're done.'

'Luke, I—' The call cut out abruptly. She *what*?

'Three minutes,' said the comm.

Pity strangling a Naval officer was a court-martial offence. Luke muttered his thanks and left the room no less conflicted than he'd entered it. He was rostered to dive again in less than an hour and once underwater the work would claim him and with it would come focus and clarity.

Meanwhile, there was far too much time available to obsess about all the things he'd wanted to say to Madeline.

And hadn't.

Six days later with the torpedo clean-up behind him, Luke put down on Guam and set about making arrangements to fly back to Singapore. He had forty-eight hours to kill before he could board a plane. Rec diving was out—never mind the bounty of shallow sunken World War Two wrecks on offer—or he'd have an even longer wait before flying, but snorkelling was in, and fishing, and waiting impatiently for time to pass, that was most definitely in.

He called Maddy again. Yun answered.

'Evening, Yun, it's Luke.'

'Greetings, tiger.'

'Maddy there?'

'No, she's at orchestra concert with new friend. Gentle rabbit good focus for snake without tiger. Gentle rabbit swift and wily, but also serene. Gentle rabbit *already* knows t'ai chi.'

'Lucky rabbit.' Luke wasn't entirely sure which world Yun inhabited sometimes. Not this one. But the gist of her words was that Madeline was out with a friend. She probably had all sorts of friends he hadn't met, both male and female, new and old. He wasn't the jealous type. Never had been. But right now he had the sinking suspicion that when it came to Madeline he might be, whether he wanted to be or not. He wanted to ask Yun for more details on the rabbit. The fact that he *didn't* pretty much made him a saint. 'Can you tell Madeline that I'm back on land in Guam, and that the job's done and I'll be back in a couple of days?'

'I can,' said Yun. 'And I might. Why more days away? Are you injured?'

'No, I just can't fly too soon after diving.'

'Good,' said Yun. 'Use time to rest, relax, and rebalance. Could also use time to acquire peace offerings for weary housekeeper and hard-pressed dojo sensei.'

'What do you mean?'

'People here not balanced when you leave. Someone have to guide them back to equilibrium while you worked. Someone doubtless have to guide them through unsettling euphoria when you return. Your fault, you fix.'

'How?'

'Do I look like a prophet to you? Rest well, tiger,' said Yun, and hung up.

Luke stepped off the jet and onto Singapore cement two days later and none the wiser as to how he was going to bring balance to the force that was Maddy and Po and Yun and Jake.

Maybe he needed to be more particular about the jobs he took on in future. Maybe if there was someone else equally qualified and available to do the work, he could let it pass him by.

Maybe *sometimes* he could do that.

But not every time.

He collected his gear and worked his way through customs—special customs conditions for him on account of his tools, but eventually the paperwork caught up with his arrival and he got the stamp he needed.

The rest of the passengers had disappeared by the time he walked through the arrival gates but a few people still stood waiting. Madeline was one of them.

She sent him an uncertain smile and fiddled with the strap of her glossy red handbag. Nervous, he thought. He could see it in her eyes as he approached.

'I thought you might need a lift,' she said when he reached her.

He dropped his bag, enfolded her in his arms and found peace the likes of which he'd never known. Not the euphoria that came of defeating death. It was quieter than that and ran deeper. He brushed his lips against her temple, not daring to take her lips. Not here. He needed privacy for what he had in mind. He needed to know that he wouldn't have to stop.

'You didn't need to come and get me,' he murmured, ridiculously glad that she had.

'See, there's where you're wrong,' she said. 'I have approximately eight hours before I hop on a plane to Shanghai, four of them in the office, and I wanted to spend as much of the other four as I could with you.'

'Eight hours, you said?' He'd worry about the why of her trip to Shanghai later.

'Four of which are yours,' she said, and stepped out of his embrace. 'How was Guam?'

He picked up his duffel and started towards the exit, preferably by way of a cash machine. 'Micronesia's lovely,' he said. 'Good diving. Even at depth. Reminded me why I went Navy in the first place.'

'You needed the reminder?' asked Maddy.

'Sometimes I do.' Damn sure he'd needed something to lift him, because putting himself on the line and waiting for the adrenalin rush to kick in certainly hadn't worked. Somewhere along the line the thrill of high stakes had been replaced by cold, hard determination to get the job done and get home. 'I need to get some money before we leave.'

'Madeline,' said an elderly voice from behind them and Madeline stopped and turned. Luke turned too. A stooped and elderly woman was walking towards them, the hand she'd extended towards Madeline dripping with jewellery and manicured to perfection. The jewellery matched the woman's clothes and the assurance with which she wore both indicated that, as far as this dame was concerned, women were never too old to showcase Cartier's finest.

'Sarah!' said Madeline with a surprisingly genuine smile as she took the outstretched hand. 'You're back in the country!'

'Just in,' said the older woman, stepping back to examine Madeline thoroughly. 'You're looking well, darling girl.' Sarah's bright blue gaze cut to Luke. 'Are you the cause?'

'Sarah, this is Luke Bennett. Luke's fresh in from disarming torpedoes in Guam, and it's possible he's part of the cause. Luke, it's my pleasure to introduce you to Lady Sarah Southcott. Sarah chairs quite a few of the charity organisations I'm involved with.'

'Lady Sarah,' said Luke.

'Just Sarah,' ordered the lady. 'Guam, eh? I did some nursing in Guam years ago.'

'Sarah spent most of World War Two nursing here in Singapore,' murmured Madeline.

'An experience I've spent a great many years trying to forget,' said the lady. 'Some of the choices we were forced to make… Terrible, terrible choices.' Her eyes took on a faraway expression and when they returned to the present they were focused on Luke. Whatever she saw there made a sad smile touch her lips. 'You look like a man who knows a thing or two about impossible choices.'

Luke said nothing. He knew of death and choices, yes, but nothing on the scale of what those in Singapore in World War Two had encountered. His respect for the bent old woman soared.

'Do you need a lift anywhere?' asked Madeline.

'No, darling girl, I have a driver here somewhere.

Apparently he's gone to collect the car and I really must go through to the pickup zone or he'll have to go around again.'

'I'll come with you,' said Madeline. 'Luke was just heading over to get some cash out. Shall I meet you back here in five?' she asked him.

Maybe Madeline wanted to talk to Sarah alone or maybe she wanted to afford him some extra privacy while he checked his finances, but whatever the reason Luke went with her suggestion and offered up a polite farewell to the formidable Sarah.

'Get Madeline to bring you over for afternoon tea sometime,' said Sarah. 'I make a mean iced tea.'

'She certainly does,' murmured Madeline. 'Long Island based with seven white spirits. Three of them gin.'

The cash machine stood near a row of car-hire places and an information service area. Luke accessed his accounts, saw that payment on this last job had come in. The balance was healthy. Enough that he could maybe think about buying himself some wheels for getting around Singapore without touching his investments. Two wheels rather than four. Far more practical in this city. And maybe he could convince Maddy to come along for the ride every now and then.

The words he heard next, while he stood there waiting for the cash and the card, came to his ears on a wind full of malice. He couldn't see the speakers. He didn't need to. He knew the type. Wealthy. Indulged. Spiteful.

'Did you see the Delacourte whore?'

'How could you not?' Another voice this time. Same toffee-nosed expat accent. 'I wonder who the pretty was?

I thought she must've been meeting him but then she left with La Southcott.'

'What's the bet she comes back for him?' said the first voice. 'I would.'

'Yeah, well, I hope he likes them well used. I heard old man Delacourte scraped her up off a street corner in Jakarta.'

'I heard that too. My father swears it's true. I also heard that, at last count, she was worth over two hundred and fifty million,' the first voice replied. 'You really think he's going to care?'

The women laughed. Luke's mind went blank as temper, molten and dangerous, threatened to erupt. Only years of rigorous military discipline stayed his hand.

'Are you ready to go?' said a voice from behind him.

Madeline, looking cool, collected and impossibly aloof.

'How much did you hear?'

'Enough.' She shot him a look he couldn't fathom. 'It's okay, I'm used to it. I'm not about to let it spoil my day.'

'Fine. Mind if I spoil theirs?' He didn't wait for an answer, just strode around the counter until he could see them. He made sure that they could see him as he committed their faces to memory. Idle malice wrapped in beauty. Madeline was worth a thousand of them.

One woman's face reddened. The other woman blanched.

Madeline came up beside him. 'Now we can go,' he muttered.

They headed from the terminal and over to the car park in silence. Luke still seething for lots of reasons, some of which he wasn't even ready to acknowledge.

It had to be the Mercedes.

Hell, he should be thankful for small mercies. She probably had a Lamborghini, a Bugatti Veyron, and an Aston Martin tucked away somewhere too.

'Would you like to drive?' she offered diffidently.

'No.' He hated to sound so curt. He hated the flinch in her eyes. He hated the thought of giving any credence whatsoever to the conversation he'd overheard, and, dammit, given time he'd sort it and stow it in the garbage where it belonged. But right now he could not.

He stowed his gear in the boot and headed for the passenger seat. He tried to rip the conversation from his mind as Madeline paid for the parking and they headed for the city. He slid a fifty-dollar note from his wallet and tucked it in her handbag. 'I pay my own way,' he said and knew his words for a mistake the minute he uttered them. He did not take them back.

'You shouldn't let what you overheard bother you,' she said eventually. 'Delacourte *is* worth hundreds of millions, yes, but I only hold a sixty-per-cent stake in the company and even at that the money stays within Delacourte. I draw down an annual director's wage of five hundred thousand—that's modest compared to what some company directors earn. I use part of that money to run my household. I have Yun, and a part-time gardener. But there's always plenty left at the end of each financial year and that money goes straight to charity.'

'You don't have to explain.'

'I know,' she said doggedly. 'But I wanted you to know that it's not as much as they said. That it's not all designer shoes and handbags for me. I don't stint when it comes to my comfort, I'm the first to admit that, but I don't spend frivolously either. There's a line between what's mine and what's Delacourte's and it's hard to explain, but it's there.'

'You don't have to explain,' he said tightly and she lapsed into silence.

The silence lasted all the way to Luke's apartment. Madeline slid into a no-parking zone. She did not stop the car.

'If it's not the money comment that bothered you there's only one other thing it can be.' She stared straight ahead as she spoke, her hands clenched around the steering wheel. 'You want to ask me about that street corner in Jakarta, Luke?'

'No.'

'Because you don't believe I could ever do such a thing?' She looked at him then. 'Or because you're afraid to?'

'Maybe I just don't like the way those poisonous women talked about you. Have you factored that into your calculations?'

'No, but I will,' she said grimly. 'I told you from the start what a lot of people think of me. Their opinions don't change—it doesn't matter what I do. So I do what I want and I do my best to ignore what people say about me behind my back. I'd suggest you do the same but I can see that's not going to work for you.'

'For heaven's sake, Maddy. What they said hurt you. Don't try and tell me it didn't.'

'It didn't. I'm used to it. You're not. Jake and Po and even Yun have protected you from what other people think of me. I tried to tell you. I warned you, over and over, but you wouldn't listen, and now you're finally seeing the whole picture and it's not what you want. The trophy wife. The Delacourte whore. The wealthy widow with more enemies than friends. Putting out for you in a lift, oh, you liked that. And now you're wondering what kind of woman would do such a thing with a man she barely knew if not a whore.'

'No.'

'Ask me if I ever whored on a street corner in Jakarta.'

'No.' His voice had taken on a clipped and dangerous edge.

'But you want to know. You think it's possible. I can see it in your eyes.'

'I don't give a damn what you think you see in my eyes, Madeline. You're wrong. I have no intention of asking you what you were doing on some street corner in Jakarta. I'm not the one harping on some throwaway comment made by a spiteful stranger. You are. So tell me whatever the hell it is you have to tell me and maybe then we can move on.'

She stared at him through dry and burning eyes, her hands not leaving the wheel. She looked as if she wanted to flee, as if she'd rather be anywhere but here with him right now. Hell of a homecoming, he thought grimly. But demons were demons and Madeline's had well and truly come out to play.

'I never sold myself on any street corner,' she said fiercely. 'But Remy did. That's where I found him. That's the life he lived and through him I knew it too. The sickness and the desperation. The crack and the hits and the marks. Does that help you to understand me any better, Luke? Or is it just one more piece of the puzzle that doesn't fit your neat and honourable little world?'

'Maybe if you stopped putting words in my mouth you'd find out,' he said grimly and opened the car door. 'Maybe if you believed in me the way you'd have me believe in you, you wouldn't be so quick to tear down the relationship we've built. Or is it simply that you've decided that you've slummed enough and want out, is that it? You'd rather hide behind all that Delacourte money and your unsavoury reputation than take a chance on falling in love—really in love—with someone like me?'

'Get out,' she muttered and released the boot where his luggage was. 'Get out of my car.'

He got out and left the car door open while he got his gear and shut the boot. He dropped his duffel on the pavement and reached for the car door again. 'You know, for all you've been through… The way you made something of yourself, your fearlessness in business, the hands-on work you do with children like Po, and the fine example your late husband set for you when it came to loving wholeheartedly no matter what other people thought… I thought you'd have more guts.'

He slammed the door.

She drove away and Luke's heart and his hopes went with her.

A single-word expletive, whorish and dirty, seemed about right.

For good measure, he said it twice.

CHAPTER TWELVE

OKAY, so maybe she had overreacted, Madeline thought heatedly as she headed for her office. Maybe Luke hadn't taken those comments to heart as much as she'd thought. But where the hell did he get *off* telling her she didn't have the guts to love him? Accusing her of sabotaging their relationship because she was afraid of where it might lead.

'The hell with you,' she muttered as she drove down into the Delacourte underground car park and headed for the lift. 'How dare you get all righteous with me? Can't even drive a damn car!'

Madeline was still fuming when she reached her office. Positively incensed at how slow her preparations for Shanghai were taking. Her fault for stopping every five minutes to remind herself that she wasn't weak or stupid for forcing a reckoning with him over her less than stellar reputation. What it was like to carry it. How it would tarnish him too. A man as honourable as Luke Bennett would object to that.

Wouldn't he?

He'd been furious about those comments. He *had*. His

ego wounded by the money and the power she wielded. His judgement questioned. It hadn't simply been protectiveness and rage on her behalf.

Had it?

Madeline sat at her desk and closed her eyes, and thought back over their conversation. Luke's fierce refusal to ask her the question. The molten fury in his eyes upon hearing those women's words. She could have given him some credit for wanting to protect her and realising he could not. A little leeway when it came to his first encounter with high-society gossip and malice. Stab you and smile and the only recourse was never to bleed out in front of them. Never show weakness. Never let on that you cared.

She could have given Luke at least some time to get his head around such a subtle form of warfare. A man used to far fiercer struggles would have had to temper his reaction. Shut it down fast rather than overreact and cause untold damage.

And he had shut down. By the time they'd reached the car he'd been as remote as a chill Antarctic wind.

Madeline swore and slumped into her desk chair and closed her eyes as she worked her way back through the conversation again, revisualising it, all of it, only this time putting a different spin on Luke's responses.

Not his fault that those women had chosen to spread their spite.

His refusal to question her about Jakarta. Not interested, not listening. La la la.

What if he really had dismissed it as not right and as far as he was concerned that was that?

What if she'd misjudged him? What if it hadn't been him pulling back and holding out this time, but her?

Madeline swore again.

Could she put the Shanghai trip on hold?

Not without horrendous ramifications for the Delacourte apartment build.

Was there time before the flight to fix things with Luke?

There was only one way to find out.

She picked up the phone and dialled his number before she lost her nerve. The phone rang out and went to voice-mail. She didn't know his other number, the one for his work phone, the one he never switched off.

She'd have to find him in person, so it was down in the lift and the car and back to his apartment, praying that he would be there.

He wasn't.

Luke showered and shaved, donned a clean set of clothes and left for Jake's. He couldn't stay in the apartment without chewing on his argument with Madeline. He couldn't think on that without starting to steam. First at the hurtful way in which the women had spoken of Madeline, and secondly at Madeline's assumption that he would believe what they'd said.

So what if momentarily he had felt intimidated by all that wealth? So what if she'd pegged his response a little too accurately in that regard? He was working through all that. William and the money, and all that came with it. He was almost there.

No, it was her ready assumption that he would believe her a whore that ate at him most. As if she thought he couldn't see exactly what she was and wasn't. As if no one but her beloved William could see her and love her no matter what.

Jake's training floor stood empty. He found them in the kitchen, eating noodles. Po smiled quick and wide. Jake looked Luke over closely before he finally summoned a greeting. 'Madeline find you at the airport?'

'Yes.'

'So why are you here?'

'Because I love you, bro. I love you so much I'm not even going to beat the happy out of you. Any more questions?'

'None that I plan to *ask*,' muttered Jake.

'I mean, I'm a reasonable human being,' said Luke, pulling up a chair. 'It's not as if my judgement's completely skewed when it comes to Madeline. I know who she is and the baggage she brings. And I sure as hell know what she's not!'

Jake kept right on eating. Po had stopped and was watching him warily.

'All right, so maybe calling her a coward wasn't the brightest thing I've ever done. Thinking I believed them when they called her a whore wasn't exactly a smart move on her part either.'

'Someone called Madeline a whore?' asked Jake, his eyes narrowing. 'Who?'

'See?' said Luke. 'You want vengeance. So did I. What's so wrong about that? It's a perfectly normal reaction.'

'Of course it is,' said Jake. 'What did you do?'

Far less than he'd wanted to do. 'They were just a pair of gossiping hags. I stared at them and then we left.'

'Reasonable,' offered Jake. 'Very civilised.'

Not altogether satisfying, brooded Luke. 'What else can you do?'

'I dare say Madeline could find plenty of ways to make their lives difficult if she wanted to, but she doesn't,' said Jake. 'She ignores them and goes her own way. There are a lot of people out there who admire her for it too—the fact that she doesn't feel the need to explain herself to anyone.'

She'd explained herself to Luke though. More than once and at his request. He remembered how he'd harped on about her relationship with William. Trying to understand it, trying to make it fit, just the way she'd accused. Maybe she did have some *slight* cause to be a little unsure of him when it came to her past and how he might interpret the things he'd overheard. Luke rubbed his palms down his face. Maybe he'd had it coming.

'They said that William Delacourte had scraped her off a street corner in Jakarta,' he muttered. 'She thought I believed them. She thought I was going to give her the third degree about it.'

No comment from the stalls.

'All right, so it took me a while to get past her marrying Delacourte, but I'm over it. That was then, this is now, dammit. Why the hell can't she trust me to see her clearly?'

'I need a holiday,' said Jake.

'Because she loves you and she's scared of what you'll think of her when people say those things that are half true and half not,' said Po. 'She's scared you'll hurt her worse than all the other times she's been hurt and that this time she won't be able to get back up.'

Jake stared at the kid. So did Luke.

'Huh,' said Jake.

'He wants to be a human rights lawyer,' said Luke.

'So I heard.' Jake eyed Luke steadily. 'He made you a gift. He's been fiddling with it for two weeks.' Jake looked to Po. 'You want to go get it?'

Po nodded and sped off. Jake eyed Luke steadily. 'You planning on being in the right frame of mind to receive it?'

'Yes,' said Luke curtly, and attempted to park his love-life woes outside the dojo door for a time.

The kid hurried back in carrying a newspaper-wrapped parcel about an inch deep, a foot or so wide, and roughly twice as tall. Po handed it to him and stepped back, just out of range. Instinctive and absolute, the physical distance Po kept from the people around him.

'Yun helped me oil and wax it,' said the boy.

Luke set the parcel on the table and ripped away the newspaper to reveal a wooden display case with brass hinges and a glass front.

'You made this?' said Luke.

Po nodded.

'Well done.' He slid his hand over the beautifully crafted edges. 'Really well done.'

'Jake said you had this medal for bravery. More than one,' said Po. 'So Maddy suggested you might like a case for them, and you could put your medals in the case and fix it to a wall somewhere it'd remind us how much other people need you too.'

'Thanks, kid.' Luke's throat felt thick and his eyes felt raw. Not tears, heaven forbid, but he didn't look up from the box for a very long time. Madeline again, smoothing his way. Making things right.

'Yun said that if you asked her nicely in Mandarin she'd come over to your place and show you where to hang it for best feng shui and she won't even charge you a consultant's fee,' said Po. 'She said you'd better have something strong to balance it, and, knowing tigers, you wouldn't.'

'It's already balanced,' said Luke quietly. 'I know it was made for me by you.' Luke looked down at the case again and ran his fingers along the oiled and waxed wood grain. 'This the kind of finish you want for the desk?'

Po nodded.

'We should make a start on that soon.'

Po nodded again, jerkily this time, and suddenly Luke's arms were full of boy. Somewhere deep inside him Luke felt one of the pieces of his life slide silently back into place as he gathered the boy in his arms and hugged him close. He looked at Jake over the small boy's head. 'I argued with Maddy. I need to find her before she leaves for Shanghai. I need to go shopping.'

'Are these statements in any way related?' asked Jake as Luke released Po and began to pace the room.

But Luke was on a roll, thinking of ways to fix what needed fixing, connecting the dots. It would start with a declaration of love, he thought. Dear heaven, he was putting his heart on the line, unconditionally and for ever, and it was so much more terrifying than merely putting up his life for the taking. Adrenalin to *burn*. Paralysing fear. 'Jewellery shopping.'

'Some little…trinket?' said Jake hopefully.

'No. Some whopping great ring. But not just any ring.

It has to be perfect. Where the hell am I going to find perfect at...' he glanced at his dive watch '...four-thirty on a Sunday afternoon in Singapore?' He knew nothing of shopping for rings. 'There's no time!' Not if he wanted to find Maddy before take-off. Which he did. 'The airport! They have jewellery stores at the airport! All right. Good. We have a location. No need to panic! Now all I need is a...a shopping companion. Preferably a female one.'

'Thank you, God,' muttered Jake.

Preferably a female with insanely romantic tendencies and a passing awareness of his increasingly fragile psyche. 'Yun! No. Not Yun. Do either of you know a gentle rabbit with a penchant for opera and who also knows t'ai chi?'

Jake blinked. Po stared.

'This is what happens when you lose your mind,' Jake told Po.

'Hallie! I could phone Hallie. She'd know what women want when it comes to engagement rings. I could describe stuff to her over the phone.' It wouldn't be ideal but it was better than nothing.

'Tris!' he said suddenly, while Jake looked on as if reluctantly fascinated by Luke's meltdown. Tris could buy Kimberley diamonds straight from the mines, and what was more Tris's wife, Erin, was a sweetheart, a romantic, and a jeweller.

He could call Erin and describe the airport rings on offer: a diamond, maybe—heaven knew, Madeline already had enough sapphires. A brilliant white diamond, set in platinum, and flowing around it a river of sapphires, just in case sapphires really were Madeline's thing. Hell, if he couldn't find what he wanted today, maybe he could commission Erin to make him something wonderful. Maybe he should be thinking along those lines *anyway*. It wasn't as if he absolutely had to have a ring for Maddy today. Given the time constraints, maybe just the words would do. With any luck Luke wouldn't have to go ring shopping at *all*.

He stopped. He beamed. He let the contentment that came of problem-solving flow over him. 'I've changed my mind,' he said.

'Of course you have,' said Jake, eyeing him as if he were a particularly unstable slab of C4.

'I'll sort the ring stuff tomorrow.'

The dojo phone rang. Jake took the call with what Luke considered unseemly haste.

'Yes, he's here,' muttered Jake. 'Where are you?'

'Is that Maddy?' said Luke. 'Give me the phone.'

'No! Get your own phone,' muttered Jake into the phone as he fended off Luke's attempts to acquire the phone. 'No, I wasn't talking to you, Maddy. You stay right where you are! There are children here. People trying to eat. Once upon a time it was even peaceful here. Besides, he was just leaving.' Luke jammed his elbow into Jake's solar plexus but his brother did not relinquish the phone. The pair of them slammed into the wall instead, Jake grinning widely now while Po cleared the bowls from the table, with a street kid's eye for impending doom. 'Maddy's at your apartment,' Jake told him, and then returned his attention to the phone. 'Yep, he'll be there in five.'

But Luke was already halfway down the hall.

'Possibly less,' said Jake, and hung up.

He found her waiting on the small landing at the top of the stairs, his door and another the only options available to her. He blocked the stairs. Madeline was going nowhere until he'd had his say.

She looked cool and unapproachable. Determined, but so was he.

'I don't care what those women think,' she said, and to hell with pleasantries. 'I care a great deal for what you think, so if you still want to pursue a relationship and see where it leads, I'm in. I have guts. I have plenty of guts.'

'I know.'

Challenge had always shaped Luke. It shaped him now as he opened his door and stepped back to let her inside.

'And self-esteem, I have that too, most of the time, only today I didn't,' she said doggedly. 'I'm sorry I over-reacted and took my insecurities out on you. I'm sorry I didn't trust you enough to blow off the comments those women made.'

'Trust has to be earned,' he said gruffly. 'I grilled you about William enough times you'd probably come to expect that I'd automatically think the worst.'

'Every time you grilled me about William you wanted to think the best of me,' she mumbled. 'But you couldn't. I made that impossible for you.'

'No. What you did was make me see you, Madeline Mercy Delacourte, for all that you are, and every time I did see you, I fell for you just that little bit more.' He took a deep breath and turned to face her. 'My turn, Maddy, to say my piece. I know I came up with some crazy philosophy about caring for each other only not too much, but, Maddy, I blew it, and there's no putting it back together because it's gone. All the way gone.'

This was where a ring would have come in handy but he didn't have a ring, he only had the words. 'I love you. I want to build a life with you. One that has room for kids like Po in it and kids of our own—we can call one William if you want, in honour of an extraordinary man. I want a life with room for Delacourte in it, and all that goes with it, and room for my work as well, and Yun's gruel, and I want you at my side, even when you can't be there in person, and I want you in my heart, because that's where you belong.'

He went to her then, stopping just in front of her to trace the curve of her brow with his fingers. God, she was trembling. So was he. 'Madeline Mercy Delacourte, I know it's a big ask, but will you marry me?'

'Yes,' she said raggedly, and kissed his cheek, and the side of his mouth, and finally his lips. 'I love you, Luke Bennett, with all that I am. For all that you are. Yes, I'll marry you.'

Home, he thought, and trembled just that little bit more as she flowed into his embrace. After all his years of restlessness and wandering he'd finally found a home for his heart. 'How many hours did you say we had before we have to get you to the airport?'

'Enough.'

Madeline phoned him two days later from her hotel room in Shanghai. Business had been concluded, she was tired beyond reckoning, and getting straight on the next plane to Singapore and stepping off it and into Luke's arms beckoned brightly. But something had come up.

'When are you coming home?' he asked, the minute he answered the phone.

'Patience, warrior. The meeting was this morning and there's a ticket on tonight's plane home with my name on it, but, Luke, I wanted to talk to you about that.' Madeline closed her eyes and flopped back on the bed. 'I went to a cocktail party with Jianne last night and I met the man she's running from and he's the worst kind of serpent. All-powerful, immoral, and twelve kinds of sly. I thought I might stick around for a couple of days and see if I can persuade Jianne to come back to Singapore with me. I think it'd be a good idea.'

'Do you need me to come to Shangahi?' offered Luke quietly.

This was how he must sound to the people he worked with, she thought with pride. Impossibly calm, instantly focused, and ready for anything. 'I'd love you to come to Shangahi,' she told him. 'For I've a powerful need for you, and it's only getting stronger. But if you're asking whether you should come here to protect Jianne, I don't think that's wise. This man doesn't see me as a threat— not yet—but he'll see you as one, and he has far too much authority here. Singapore would be better. And he *will* come for her, Luke. He's not going to go away.'

'Don't you *dare* put yourself in danger or, so help me, Madeline—'

'You know, that's rich,' she interrupted wryly. 'Coming from you. Welcome to my world, warrior. Wallow in it a while and then we'll talk. I'll show you a coping mechanism or two that I picked up while you were pulling apart warheads in Guam. One of them was to believe, with all my heart, that you knew what you were doing, and that you were the best man for the job.'

Silence.

'Now you're angry with me,' said Madeline on a sigh. 'Does this mean we get to have wild, angry make-up sex when I get back? Because, you know, I'm all in.'

'Madeline,' he said tightly. 'Just get here safely. Let me worry about the intricacies of the sex.'

'Control freak.'

'Control's not really going to have a lot to do with it,' he said, and a promise was born. 'You *call* me as you're getting on the plane, do you hear me? I'll meet you at the airport.'

'Impatient,' she said.

'Protective,' he countered. 'And by the time I see you next there's every likelihood in the world I'll be insane. Do *not* take stupid risks. If the situation comes unstuck you go to ground and you *call* me and you wait for me to come for you.'

'I have this insatiable urge to salute you,' she murmured. 'Why is that? Did you have some kind of high-falutin' Naval rank I should know about, or should I just call you sir?'

Luke hung up on her after that. She guessed it was going to be wild, angry make-up sex after all. Madeline put the phone back in its cradle, shed her high-powered businesswoman clothes, and wriggled her way down between the thousand–thread-count sheets and a duvet lighter than air.

She closed her eyes and figured the timing good for a couple of hours' sleep if she tried—Lord knew she was tired enough. She willed her body to relax and smiled as faintly, on the whisper of a warm jungle wind, she thought she heard a thwarted tiger roar.

Two days later, Madeline and Jianne touched down in Singapore. They were met by Jianne's cousins—Bruce Yi's sons—and, by the looks on their faces and the way they flanked her and Jianne as they made their way from the airport and into the waiting chauffeur-driven Mercedes, neither of them were to be discounted when it came to protecting their own. They treated Madeline as their equal, with a newfound respect that had nothing to do with the way she conducted business and everything to do with her getting Jianne out of Shanghai unnoticed and unintercepted.

They saw Madeline to her door, Jianne with them, as they made their farewells.

'You have the numbers I gave you?' Madeline asked Jianne. 'Luke's number and the number for the dojo. Jake's cell phone and mine. They're not just in your phone, they're in your pocket too, yes? And you're going to memorise them.'

'For the thousandth time, *yes*,' said Ji.

'You need any help, you *call* us, you hear?' said Madeline fiercely as she gave Jianne a hug.

'I hear,' said Jianne with a rosebud smile.

'And if you ever feel like heading out for a meal or to watch a movie, call me.'

Jianne assured her she would.

When they'd left, Madeline showered and dried her hair and applied make-up, and as she stood in her walk-in-wardrobe and studied the clothes on offer she phoned Luke.

'I'm back,' she said lazily. 'We caught an earlier flight than the one we had planned, Jianne's cousins picked us up from the airport, and I'm currently standing in my cupboard and wondering what to wear.'

'I'll be right there,' he said. 'And there's really no need for you to worry about clothes.'

Oh, but there *was*.

Some moments in a woman's life required careful preparation and this was one of them.

'I realised something while you were away,' she said, searching through the dress racks for something short and tight and guaranteed to blow a man's mind.

An amber silk sheath had potential. Strapless. Hidden zip down the side. Add a pair of silk stockings, suspenders, and high-heeled shoes and maybe…almost inevitably…a hungry tiger would bite. Hair up or hair down? What to do?

'Hello?' said Luke. 'Madeline, would you please ignore the clothes and finish the sentence? I'm dying here.'

'Oh. Sorry.' She'd been *neglecting* him. 'I realised what a wonderful father you'd make. I realised how much I wanted to watch you come over all protective with your daughters. Those poor, poor girls.'

'Bennett boys do not beget girls,' he said firmly. 'We do boys. Guts-and-glory-driven boys.'

'No, Yun, said our firstborn was going to be a girl and

then boys after that.' Oh, this was going to be fun. 'Luke? Are you still there?'

'Do *not* leave that cupboard,' he muttered.

'Yun's not here,' she countered. '*Someone's* going to have to let you in. Oh, and, Luke?' She waited until she figured she had his full attention. 'Take the lift.'

Fifteen minutes later Luke stood in the lobby of Madeline's apartment block and set his hand to the button of Madeline's private lift. The lift came down empty, and he stepped into that mirrored space and willed the doors shut. The lift carried him smoothly upwards as he leaned back against the wall and waited with barely leashed impatience, hands to the rails, as the elevator slid noiselessly to a stop.

He had a ring in his pocket, a flawless white diamond set in platinum and surrounded by sapphires. His sister-in-law Erin had taken his commission, listened to his stuttered words on what he wanted, and somehow seen the picture in his mind and the promise in his heart and given it shape.

Once upon a time he'd lived for challenge and danger. He still did. He always would. Not altogether tamed, but love he could do, and love Madeline he did, and the knowledge that she loved him in return filled his soul.

Madeline waited restlessly, her amber sheath clinging, and every muscle vibrating with anticipation as the light above the lift came on and those silver doors slid slowly open.

He stood leaning against the back wall, tiger's left

claw and keeper of her heart, with his head thrown back, his hands to the railing, and his eyes a simmering cauldron of tender possession, reckless promise, and desire.

Madeline looked down…down to where a lady really shouldn't look.

And smiled.

HARLEQUIN *Presents*

Coming Next Month

from **Harlequin Presents®**. Available November 23, 2010.

Coming Next Month

from **Harlequin Presents® EXTRA.** Available December 7, 2010.

HPECNM1110

LARGER-PRINT BOOKS!

HARLEQUIN *Presents*

PASSION
GUARANTEED
SEDUCTION

GET 2 FREE LARGER-PRINT NOVELS PLUS 2 FREE GIFTS!

HARLEQUIN®

A *Romance*

FOR EVERY MOOD™

Spotlight on

Classic

Quintessential, modern love stories
that are romance at its finest.

See the next page
to enjoy a sneak peek from
the Harlequin® Romance series.

*See below for a sneak peek from our classic
Harlequin® Romance® line.*

Introducing DADDY BY CHRISTMAS by Patricia Thayer.

MIA caught sight of Jarrett when he walked into the open lobby. It was hard not to notice the man. In a charcoal business suit with a crisp white shirt and striped tie covered by a dark trench coat, he looked more Wall Street than small-town Colorado.

Mia couldn't blame him for keeping his distance. He was probably tired of taking care of her.

Besides, why would a man like Jarrett McKane be interested in her? Why would he want to take on a woman expecting a baby? Yet he'd done so many things for her. He'd been there when she'd needed him most. How could she not care about a man like that?

Heart pounding in her ears, she walked up behind him. Jarrett turned to face her. "Did you get enough sleep last night?"

"Yes, thanks to you," she said, wondering if he'd thought about their kiss. Her gaze went to his mouth, then she quickly glanced away. "And thank you for not bringing up my meltdown."

Jarrett couldn't stop looking at Mia. Blue was definitely her color, bringing out the richness of her eyes.

"What meltdown?" he said, trying hard to focus on what she was saying. "You were just exhausted from lack of sleep and worried about your baby."

He couldn't help remembering how, during the night, he'd kept going in to watch her sleep. How strange was that? "I hope you got enough rest."

She nodded. "Plenty. And you're a good neighbor for

coming to my rescue."

He tensed. Neighbor? *What neighbor kisses you like I did?* "That's me, just the full-service landlord," he said, trying to keep the sarcasm out of his voice. He started to leave, but she put her hand on his arm.

"Jarrett, what I meant was you went beyond helping me." Her eyes searched his face. "I've asked far too much of you."

"Did you hear me complain?"

She shook her head. "You should. I feel like I've taken advantage."

"Like I said, I haven't minded."

"And I'm grateful for everything…"

Grasping her hand on his arm, Jarrett leaned forward. The memory of last night's kiss had him aching for another. "I didn't do it for your gratitude, Mia."

Gorgeous tycoon Jarrett McKane has never believed in Christmas—but he can't help being drawn to soon-to-be-mom Mia Saunders! Christmases past were spent alone…and now Jarrett may just have a fairy-tale ending for all his Christmases future!

Available December 2010, only from Harlequin® Romance®.